BOOK EIGHT OF THE
RIM CONFEDERACY

Eons
Semester

by Jim Rudnick

Cover art by Lasse Perala

ISBN-13: 978-1-988144-10-8
Copyright © 2016
Jim Rudnick

RUDNICK PRESS

For my Susan...

The RIM Confederacy: Eons Semester

"Jilted by his Royal fiancee, captain Tanner Scott is assigned to Eons and the newly constructed RIM Naval Academy buildings and the duty is anything but a reward. His days are full of squabbling University professors and construction types all nitpicking for changes to plans and additions and extra and the attention to detail is a horrible side-effect.

As he learns, there is more to looking after a successful construction project than being at the top of the heap and the machinations of the Issians who run Eons and it's mind-readers comes to him for help. He knows that the Baroness is somehow also involved but the openness of the Master Adept and her Inner Circle that controls Eons is what is so surprising to him.

As the Naval Academy is finally ready to open and the heads of state of many of the RIM Confederacy planets arrive, the protesters against the Issians make their play to publicly humiliate the Inner Circle and their own plans to strengthen their ranks via the death of twins and Tanner must find a way to quell the uprising..."

A Message to you from the Author...

I just wanted to say thanks so so much for reading Book Eight of the RIM Confederacy!

As my Amazon bio says, being a youngster in the 1950's meant that I was a voracious reader in what has been called the Golden Age of Science Fiction. That meant that for me, my heroes were not on the hockey rink or gridiron - but instead in my local Library where at 12 I had a full Adult card (thanks Dad!) and took out more than 5 books a week.

Everyone from Heinlein, Norton, Leiber, Pohl, Anderson, Simak, Asimov, Brackett, Gunn, Van Vogt and more....I fell in love with and eventually owned Ace Doubles of my own.

4

And while I never knew who wrote the Tom Corbett - Space Cadet series, I fell in love with them and they had a place of honor on my own bookcase too!

With that kind of an introduction to Science Fiction, it's no wonder that when I got my writing work done, I turned my own fictional side of my brain to writing same. It's one thing I know how to write - and a totally different matter to release same to the world - something that I've just started to work on....

Suffice it to say my own works are rooted in that Golden Age and it's that era that I'd like to one day be known as a teensy contributor to in some small way...

So once again, thanks for beginning my RIM Confederacy series and wait'll you learn about the alcoholic spaceship captain that is my hero, who fights and beats aliens but not the bottle!

Enjoy and remember, in a series, characters develop and mature not the way we sometimes want...instead, it's like they have a life of their own!

And while you can read the series in any

order, I'd highly recommend to start with Pirates, then Sleeper Ship, Prison Planet, Ancient Relics, Hospital Ship, Desert Planet, Ruined Memories and Eons Semester too...and yes, there's more coming soon too!

Prologue ~

On Tavira, the moon that lay above Eons, an Issian lay in restraints in a secure medical ward in the capital city of Aporia. The Issian sometimes fought them, but they were too tight to give even a millimeter. She was a youngish woman in her thirties, but she had long ago given up any kind of care and concern for her looks and her body. Half-conscious and always in a drug-induced stupor, the woman lay quietly on the bed.

Her hair, now tangled, knotted, and even missing in some spots along one temple, should have been blonde but was now brown with dried blood and pus from an open sore. Her hair hadn't been washed in months.

Her toenails and fingernails were long, curled and dull yellow as the keratin was thick and unkempt. If anyone ever came close enough, she would try to rake them with those nails. But that was before the medication dosages were upped, and she hadn't tried that in weeks.

Her teeth were once shiny and white but now were yellow and brittle. A few were missing; for some reason, she would worry a tooth with her tongue and do that long enough and often enough that she would spit out a tooth onto the plain steel ward floor. They fed her via a gastric feeding tube

7

that had been inserted through a small incision in the abdomen into the stomach and was used for long-term enteral nutrition. She hadn't tasted food in almost a year, but she didn't care.

Her eyes were light blue but such a light tone as to be almost white; each had a huge iris that took up almost the whole of the eyeball—the coal black pupils were large too. Staring at her many had found was treacherous—one could easily fall right into her brain some said. And what a brain it was— she was an Issian twin with all the anxiety that that might mean.

Her gown, if it could be called that, lay on her frame like an old tarpaulin on rough ground. She had the usual female parts but not one could be called a curve.

She was anything but attractive—in fact, she was anti-attractive to anyone who could see the real woman.

Of course, that never happened up here in the Issian Secure Ward.

No one came.

No one visited.

No one cared.

In fact, for a full sixty feet around this ward room, no one was usually allowed to enter except the medical robo drones the ward staff used to tend to her. Once a week, an Issian doctor attended who read charts and nodded but did nothing else.

There was nothing to do—she was a twin.

And now change was coming, and as yet, no plans had been made for this twin.

CHAPTER ONE

Stepping onto the boarding dock of the *Nugent* shuttle, Tanner stopped for a moment to turn and speak to some of his crew, who'd followed him to see him off.

"Fellows—well, and girls too," Tanner said as he included Lieutenant Irving who'd come along even though her replacement was not even on station back on the bridge, "this is not goodbye—but a simple see you all soon!" He smiled even though he knew something was definitely wrong with his new mission to Eons.

"Sir," Kondo said, "this is a mistake—I intend to ask for a full investigation on this, Sir—even if I have to go to the Barony Captain's Council at gunpoint."

He was upset and a part of that, Tanner knew,

was that their own plans of beating the invader mother ship had just worked—and now his captain was getting sent elsewhere.

"Kondo, stand down, lad," Tanner said quietly. "Nothing to be gained by raising the hackles on others—find out what you must, but always act politely—works best I've found," he finished off.

Bram held out his hand to shake, and Tanner grasped it and shook it gladly.

"If I can—and I'd think I might need help—I'll ask that you get moved over to Eons too for a spell, Bram," Tanner said, and his mind sent a be safe and well thought to his Adept officer.

The bond between them had been forged in too many instances for them to forget what each meant to the other, and the Issian gave Tanner a firm and heartfelt hug.

He shook hands with Irving, Sheldon, and then Cooper, grinned at them, and said, "If we're all here, who'n the hell is running the *Atlas*?"

They all laughed loudly. AI had been kicked in as the *Atlas* lay off KappaD in low orbit, and the ship was in no trouble at all.

He smiled. "Gotta go, be good one and all."

Tanner turned and marched up the landing ramp into the *Nugent* shuttle and took a seat quickly, as he faced away from the still open port, not wanting the crew to see his face. He was not happy, but sadly, as he well knew, the job of being a Navy captain often meant orders that were not so much fun. Like this time.

He'd been seconded from the captaincy of the *BN Atlas* to immediately transfer to Eons and take part in the new Barony Naval Academy facility merge under Rear Admiral Ethan Higgins, who was in charge of the program.

And once those duties were complete, he would remain on Eons at the Navy Academy as an adjunct professor for the first Semester of their academic year; his orders were signed by the Baroness herself.

Wonder what that's all about—wait, he thought.

"The Lady St. August perhaps ..." he said to himself and shook his head as the most probable reason why he'd just been taken off space duty and sent to a landlocked menial job presented itself.

The shuttle pilot looked back at him and questioned, "Are we good to go, Captain?"

Tanner nodded while he remembered Lady St. August's soft, soft skin, how she looked, how she felt, and more. His change of their relationship was the most likely reason for his exile.

He was being exiled to a planet of mind readers because he wanted to get a better hold of their chances of a successful life together rather than what he imagined it would be like being a Royal.

He shook his head one more time.

Eons. New duty station. Help Higgins to build the new Academy and then teach at same. That sounded okay. Boring. But okay. Dumb-ass. But okay. He snorted.

The pilot was good, and the quick shuttle flight to the *Nugent* was done in minutes. As the craft touched down on the *Nugent* landing port deck, Tanner got up and went down the ramp to greet a small group of officers who appeared to be waiting for him.

"Captain Scott," a lieutenant commander said as he stepped forward, "could we welcome you to the *Nugent* and then ask you to follow us to meet with the admiral in our ready room, Sir?"

Tanner nodded and no introductions were offered or made, so he trooped in with the others. They made their way down the central corridor to the lift. Going up to Deck Fifty from Deck Four where the landing bays were took almost a full minute, and yet not a single one spoke—all eyes were locked onto the slowly climbing floor numbers in the lift display over the door. The chimes at fifty sounded as the doors opened, and they walked right out and onto the bridge.

Like all destroyers, this was a big bridge with the standard consoles and sections, but it also had a larger temporary area where other functions were often done that held seating and benches.

He looked at the captain's chair and caught Captain Siegel's eye. Captain Siegel half-smiled but did not turn to face him; instead, he kept on working on his console.

So, like that, Tanner thought. *Least I know where I stand here.*

He looked at the accompanying lieutenant commander and said quietly, "And the ready room is …"

The lieutenant commander pointed a finger to a closed door well across the bridge.

Tanner made his way toward same, and when he reached the door, it opened.

Inside, sitting at the conference table, sat Admiral McQueen with a stack of folders, files, and tablets. He looked up at Tanner and smiled. Full smile. It was the kind of smile that meant hello friend, and Tanner smiled back in kind.

"Tanner—please have a seat. We have some stuff to go over—but tell me first, whose cup did you piss in, lad?"

Tanner nodded. "Sir—good to see you in person, Admiral. And the cup appears to be owned by the Lady St. August," he said and sighed at the same time.

With a faraway look in his eye, the admiral slowly nodded back. "You've had what I'd call a stormy relationship with that woman for years, as I remember. But surely, this yanking of your space-duty ticket—oh, wait. More than stormy, right?"

The admiral had obviously connected the dots and that made it easier to explain but not easier either, Tanner thought.

"Sir, yes—we have known each other for years, and it's been a slowly growing relationship that—well, Sir, no stories out of school, but one that grew to be an intimate one. 'Til a week ago or so—when I asked for some kind of rationale for us to go forward, for some kind of map to follow, as I didn't want to become a Royal was my own bottom line, Sir. And that didn't go over so well, Sir," he said as he remembered the half-empty bottle of wine flying over his head.

The admiral grinned. "So, our captain wanted to stay in the navy, I take it, and not become someone to whom others bowed. Like my own choice would have been, but that didn't go over well ..." he said and chuckled. "So, Eons then. Okay, here's the skinny, lad," he said, and he tucked into the stack of folders in front of him.

As he read off the topic, he'd open up a folder, note that the status report on same was up to date, and then, with no discussion on the topic at all, simply hand the folder to Tanner.

The stack in front of him grew, and Tanner heard

only snippets of the various items.

Tower Number One had issues with shopping rental spaces—various RIM members wanted space and there just wasn't enough the admiral said. Tanner would have to handle that issue along with missing laundry equipment and residence furniture issues too. Tower Number Two held the classrooms and that was a total mess, the admiral admitted, his eyebrows soaring as he listed off the missing desks and chairs and the library without books and the lecture theaters with no stairs … and he sighed. Tower Number Three was the academy quartermaster goods and services area, and it too appeared to be a mess. Tower Number Four, the last tower that was supposed to hold academy administration with the offices for the registrar, deans, and others, wasn't even issued occupancy permits yet as many items were not within code.

The admiral sighed. "We've got Rear Admiral Higgins on this—we seconded him in from Halberd —you'd have met there, I believe?"

Tanner nodded. He'd met Higgins and actually liked the man, but he remembered that he was a micro-manager, and this whole academy building program sounded like a details job. Just the right man for the job—and now, I'm his helper, Tanner though and he smiled.

"Yes, Sir, know the man. Liked him too," he said.

The admiral raised his eyebrows again. "Remember, he's in charge, Scott. But yes, do help him out—this whole move from the older academy on the other side of Dessau to the new four towers facilities is more than any one man can handle. Help is needed," he said, and he placed the final folders on the tall pile in front of Tanner. He added a tablet to same with information about Tanner's academy ID and the facilities.

The admiral smiled. "Tanner, I was so glad to hear that you'd—well, thrown the booze out of your life. Well done. Made me proud to have called you a friend once more. And your plan on how to help us with the invader reaper ships just a few days ago showed me that I was not wrong. Welcome back—well, you're still a captain in the Barony Navy, but still, on Eons you'll be posted to the RIM Navy under Higgins. But one word of warning, Captain?" he said softly.

Tanner nodded and looked directly at his admiral.

"Royals play hardball, Tanner—so be very, very careful with the Lady St. August. She can wreck your career in an instant—or reward it too. Be cautious is what I preach—you've already gone past where I'd have drawn the line, so just be careful, son," he said, and he laid a hand down over Tanner's for a moment and patted him twice.

He nodded one more time. "So, quarters down on Deck Forty-Nine, see the deck steward for info, but your bags came over earlier, I think. Normal RIM Navy rules here on the *Nugent*—we're due into Juno in about twenty-two days or so—and there'll be an academy ship there to take you out to Eons," he said and grinned.

"Welcome back, lad …"

#####

The time on Juno was quick, Tanner thought, and he was sorry he didn't even get a chance to visit that favorite little pub he'd spent hours in, drinking his Black Scotch and looking at the Randi waterfall pictures up on the walls. He had spent one night only on the Juno Naval Base in officer's quarters and had been awakened by his wrist PDA. It chimed and then notified him his trip out to Eons on the academy training ship, the frigate the CS *Columbia*, was fueling up and he had less than two hours to get on board.

He grunted, rolled over, and then slowly arose to get to the showers and find a clean uniform. He was a bit surprised at first to find his worn uniform—the one he'd shipped in to Juno on the *Nugent*—freshly cleaned and pressed and hanging on the back of the door to his quarters. Barony captain's uniform, clean and ready to wear. He smiled, thinking that the stewards here on Juno were top-notch too, and got dressed. He'd brought his toilet bag, so combing his hair was easy this morning, and he looked into the mirror above the sink that lay in the head area of his single-room billet.

Not at all like his thousands of feet of space in the captain's quarters back on the *Atlas*, but it was still serviceable, clean, and ably stewarded. He smiled and the crinkle of his skin at the corner of his blue eyes crinkled even more. Gray hair at his temples made him realize that life was just getting interesting at forty. Life as a single navy captain, he meant, and he forced out any thoughts of Helena at the same time.

He tossed his meager belongings into the overnight satchel and threw the strap over his shoulder. He left quarters and went down the hallway to the escalator down to grade level. Outside, he asked a sergeant, who was just entering, how he could get over to the landing fields. The sergeant pointed at a metro bus just loading a few feet away.

He looked at Juno as the bus went along and thought milk run as the bus stopped often to pick up and drop off riders. Towers were few here in the naval areas, but in the close distance, the downtown major city of Juno lay well across the horizon. As the capital city of the RIM Confederacy, with more than forty realms, it was a hub of one kind or another. Each of those realms had embassies, and each had its own groupings of inhabitants.

Diversity was surely a Juno thing, he thought, as he noted that three Ttseens got on the bus and sat together across one of the seats. Ahead of them was a Leudi. Behind them on the other side of the bus sat two couples of Skoggians, their purple-colored skin almost glowing in the morning sunshine on Juno.

After another dozen stops, the driver looked up into his rearview mirror and said, "Captain, all out next stop for the Juno landing base, Sir—hard to starboard is the way to go," and he smiled as the bus came to a stop.

Jumping off the last step and waving his thanks to the driver, Tanner looked to his right and saw a Jeep waiting there with a corporal at the wheel.

"Sir—need a lift over to the port?" the corporal asked, and Tanner nodded.

As the Jeep took off, Tanner watched as the enormous fenced gates ahead grew closer and then parted. The Jeep must have initiated some kind of AI response, and they pulled up at the now erect barrier. A marine came out, looked at the corporal, and then checked Tanner's orders, which he'd handed to the man, and smiled.

"Sir, your paperwork is in order—Corporal, drop

the captain over at the *Columbia* on pad twenty-four
STAT!" He saluted as he pressed the button to raise
the barrier. Moments later, Tanner stood at the foot
of the landing escalator that went up into the
academy frigate. He was met by a bored sergeant
and two academy student officers.

"Sir, your papers ple—" the one student said and
stopped as Tanner thrust same into the young
man's hands.

He leafed through them, nodded, then made
some kind of an entry on the tablet he carried, and
handed Tanner back his orders.

"Sir, you're checked in—all the way to Eons, Sir.
Please report to the bridge after you have taken
over your quarters on Deck Twenty-Nine, Sir.
Bridge is up on Deck Thirty, Sir, if you're unaware
of how a frigate is laid out. Sir," he said.

The sergeant stifled a guffaw. "Cadet Lieutenant,
this is Captain Scott—who probably knows more
about frigates than you do the back of your hand.
Welcome, Sir," the sergeant said and snapped a
salute, which was quickly copied by the two
academy student officers.

Tanner nodded, smiled, and said, "Not a
problem, Sergeant. Will quarter up first and then
see my way to the bridge." He saluted back to the
threesome.

Quarters he found were fine—someone had

billeted him in a single, and he noted his bags from the *Atlas* stood in a row off to one side. Normal bunk, separate head, view-screen, console, and AI leads. Same as always, and he left his quarters to take the stairs up one flight to the bridge deck.

With more than one hundred and thirty crew members and about thirty officers, the *Columbia* was a normal frigate—except it was a split between navy men as supervisors and academy students in training. For all positions, Tanner knew the students in their fourth and final academy year worked out in the various navies across the RIM Confederacy. Each had a series of postings through all the major sections like the bridge, engineering, science, and ordnance, and each required that they hit a threshold of skill and experience the academy valued. If someone failed to live up to those expectations, they had to repeat that section—but the repeats were limited to one. If you failed twice to get past the section thresholds, you washed out of the academy.

Not, Tanner thought, that the washouts lost completely, as he knew of a few who had found positions with smaller Confederacy member navies in some kind of positions—but not the kind of navy men or women he'd want looking out for his back either.

He stopped at the bridge door, and as it opened,

he stepped out onto the bridge deck floor.

Ahead of him lay the normal frigate bridge, but it was slightly modified as most of the consoles had two seats laid out beside each other—one for the student and one for the supervisor. "Made sense," he said to himself, "in that the console and data were available to both for their input and feedback."

He took the few steps over to the captain's chair and snapped off a salute.

"Sir, Captain Scott reporting in and that I'm squared away, Sir," he said, and as the frigate captain turned to him, Tanner smiled.

Captain Darnell smiled back, returned the salute, and then got up to hug him.

"Tanner, so good to see you again," Darnell said, and he yanked a chair over beside him and pushed Tanner down into same.

They had been shipmates back on the RN Kerry before the pirates had attacked. Both had been very much involved in the attack on the Kerry, and Lieutenant Darnell had moved up the chain of command nicely.

"Captain," Tanner said, "you're a captain now and the *Columbia* is yours—nicely done, Tim" he said and smiled.

Tim Darnell smiled back, and yet Tanner could tell the smile was not really all there.

"Tanner—yes, thanks. And I know that you might be thinking why be a captain on an academy training frigate—and the answer is quite simple. The attack on the Kerry somehow made me realize that the life of a swashbuckling navy man was not for me—not as much as moving over to the academy side of things. I trained for a full year as a commander on an academy cruiser and then got this posting on the *Columbia* as full captain. And its pretty easy duty—Juno to Eons and back to Juno. And more importantly, least to my way of thinking, I am helping train the next class of navy men and women at the same time. Works for me, Tanner," he said and smiled that smile once more.

Tanner had a fleeting thought that such duty would never put the man in harm's way, but he stifled that thought and rightfully so. One can't measure one man's courage from another man's standards.

He clasped Tim on the arm, smiled, and said, "So, how's this bridge crew, Captain?"

Some of the supervisors around him chuckled.

Tim went through the introductions, and after about a half dozen, Tanner begged off, finding it difficult to remember who was who and what console they were running.

Tanner noted the friendly attitude between supervisors and trainees. Light and easy, he thought, which in a training environment was a good thing. Of course, there were meant to be times to test the students too, in the heat of battle as it were, but that would be a lesson for another day.

As he settled into life on the *Columbia*, he was glad to see, from his own point of view, the overall teaching and supervising were being very well done.

"Nothing like an academy grad," he said to himself and smiled.

#####

In the flyer, Tanner was a bit lost at first. Normally, the pilot held a stick or some kind of piloting device that allowed the user to direct the craft—but on these Eons flyers, the pilot used what might be called a trackball. Placed in the same spot as the stick would have been, between the pilot's legs, it was mounted to the dashboard and the solid arm was immovable. The center held a movable ball which the pilot used to direct the craft for the normal roll control. Side-to-side ball movements controlled yaw, or the direction the flyer actually took over the ground. And pitch or up-and-down controls were handled by simply changing the throttles located at the side of that ball.

He smiled after noticing same and said, "Interesting controls—have they not heard of a stick here on Eons?"

The sergeant smiled. "Sir, not on Eons—everything is the same but different somehow," he said.

He gently moved the ball and throttles at the same time, and the two-man flyer moved up and to the left. Leaving the Dessau landing fields, Tanner had requested a quick flight over to the new academy towers and the sergeant off the *Columbia* had been quick to comply.

The flyer was now almost three thousand feet above the landing port. The sergeant swung her to port, and the flyer accelerated quickly to full speed.

"She does like half a Mach," he offered.

The flyer quickly began to cover ground as the city behind them fell away and the foothills and canyons off the mountains in the distance became more visible. As the flyer hit some turbulence, the sergeant modified his speed down a notch, slowly spun the craft to its left, and picked up a river below them. It twined its way deeper and deeper into the growing canyon that angled back and forth, as it went toward the now closer mountains. In less than ten minutes, the four academy towers sprung up in the near distance.

Each was a true tower—some architect had made sure of that—and Tanner thought about form over function for a moment and then shrugged. *Different streets for different feets was the universal answer to all.*

Each tower was about four hundred feet tall, or about forty stories, he reckoned. Each tower appeared to have ground level landing ports as well as the same about midway up their expanse. Each was capped with simple arrays that he thought would handle networks, communications, and Ansible functions. He thought the apparent lack of windows of any kind was odd, and he said so to the sergeant.

"Sir, yes ... that's what it looks like—but inside you'd see that there are windows all the same—just that they're hidden from outside. Each holds like thirty-some odd floors, and each is wholly self-contained we were told. Each has its own power plant, networks, communication, and such, and at this point, they should have been issued occupancy permits. Course, guess that's why you're here, right, Sir?" he said, putting the question right out front.

"Don't know what I can do to help on that front," Tanner said, and he meant it.

The towers were all beautiful, clinging to the sides of the canyon, two on one side and two on the other side. The outer skins of the towers were dull grayish metals that glowed in the late afternoon dusky sunlight. Each was also, he noted dryly, tended by robo-welders that sparked with their tasks. One had a side-mounted set of scaffolding still erected so that meant work too, he figured. One farther away had some kind of flyers tending to the top arrays, which made Tanner give up looking for issues. There'd be plenty.

"Swing her around all four, slowly if possible," he said to the sergeant, and he complied.

Not much more could be seen, but down at ground levels, Tanner saw massive lineups of trucks and stacks of containers that were slowly being forklifted onto conveyor belts that entered the towers themselves.

"Still being worked on, for sure," he said to himself and nodded to the sergeant.

"Okay, thanks for the flyby, Sergeant. Now, please, back to Dessau and the landing field—I will need to see Rear Admiral Higgins, I expect." He leaned back as the sergeant pushed down on the throttles and the flyer leaped away from the towers.

Ahead the city of Dessau slowly grew, and while it held less than half a million inhabitants under the big blue sun, it was the capital city. That big blue sun was brighter than most, so the climate here was hot and dry. For almost three generations, the ground had been able to support less and less vegetation, and crops had long since died. No matter what kind of fertilizers had been developed, the land could not grow enough food to support the people of Eons.

It had not always been so; records going back ten centuries showed that once this had been a fertile continent with many farms and cities and commerce too. Towns had sprung up and prospered centuries ago, and the whole region was known to be an agricultural success.

But as every Issian knew, the change in their blue sun with its varying radiation meant that droughts had come and the soil had dried up for almost three centuries now, as did the economy, and the farmers left and fled to the cities and towns.

The giant blue star that Eons revolved around was young. It was still trying to find a balance, the scientists said, and the radiation would be dynamic for a while and then eventually decrease, the climate would settle, and agriculture could begin again. To support themselves, the people of Eons had done what anyone else would have done; they found ways to trade what they could for food and commerce.

In the meantime, Eons had done well with being the home of the RIM Confederacy Naval Academy, and it was amply repaid for that. This brand new academy, partially paid for by the Barony as they folded up their own academy on Neres and all was in the process of being moved to Eons, was also going to help Eons survive too.

#####

Tanner thought about the phrase déjà vu one more time and then shrugged. He'd been here before only on a different planet and years ago. It felt so much like he was re-living the past that he wondered what might happen if he got up and just left the offices and went for a Scotch. Wait. Scotch was a part of that past, no longer a part of his present, and he smiled.

Here in the administrative wing of the Eons landing port, it seemed the admiral had obviously used his rank to get an office.

And at the desk ahead of him, working on something that was obviously frustrating as hell, sat Administrative Assistant Lieutenant Kelsey CoSharan, the rear admiral's number two, and he looked upset, which for a Faraway alien was an easy tell.

Faraway aliens looked like few other races with a tail that protruded more than four feet behind them and rested often on the ground. They could leap almost thirty feet, and their race looked almost kangaroo-like with the huge legs and muscled calves; however, the tail was the best way to read a Faraway.

A stiff, unbending tail meant the alien was not going to engage, not going to work with their peers.

Yet a soft tail that would simply drop to the floor and lie still with little twitches meant that the owner was going to be approachable and work with you, it was said. And a tail that curled up, toward the alien's head, meant it was pissed.

Just like now.

Tanner smiled at the alien and continued to smile, as the assistant looked up every few minutes.

He'd sat here now for over a half hour and he wondered—

The box on the assistant's desk chimed three times, and the lieutenant looked up once more to Tanner.

"You may go right in, Captain. And welcome to Eons," he added with a wry voice. At least that's what Tanner read into it, and that curled tail still meant something else, he was sure.

He entered the inner office and found Rear Admiral Ethan Higgins, sitting at his desk, with two side tables pushed up close that were all covered with stacks and stacks of folders, files, and tablets some of which were chiming and unanswered too.

The admiral stood and came around his desk the other way to offer his hand, which Tanner took, and they shook quickly.

"Heard that you've overcome your previous … um … previous shortcomings. Good for you and the RIM Navy," he said as he sat in his chair.

"Captain, truly welcome. We need you—I've asked the admiral for help for over six months, and you're a welcome sight. Sit, please—Kelsey, get in here!" he barked.

Even though Tanner had closed the door behind him, it opened a moment later and the admiral's assistant came in—a stack of folders loaded with files in one hand and three tablets in the other. Without any direction from the admiral, he dropped the items into Tanner's lap and left the room a few seconds later.

"Not a lot of time we have—nor for that matter does the academy have to get finished, get our occupancy permits, and then take on students in the upcoming semester. We have four months is all. We, you'll note I said we, as I now count you in on the team. A team of two—well, three if you count Kelsey. You might have thought that the academy itself would be on the team—but it's them that we're fighting with daily, it seems. Course, that's why you're here—I do hope you enjoy their deans who want accent walls in their offices to hold not Randi waterfalls but a photo of their own world. Or chairmen who want their desks to be elevated so that they can look down on all who enter their offices, but somehow they want that to be hidden. Which is why I work outta here—oh, you'll see what I mean when you visit your own office over in Tower Four. But don't get too sidetracked by the various professors who hate blue boards in their lecture theaters and want them to be green or black … whatever, Captain," he said like an outpouring of his latest frustrations had boiled over.

Tanner nodded. "Sir, are we using any kind of rules of engagement to well, sort of to triage these requests and such? How important is it that a classroom blackboard be green as opposed to blue?" he asked.

The admiral nodded. "Not bloody important at all, but we can't say that to the academy staff. They must feel that their input is appreciated, I've been told by everyone from Admiral McQueen to the Confederacy Council to the Master Adept. Yet we still gotta get it all done in four more months. You'll be hard pressed I know to nod to a professor about his concerns, while mentally saying no chance to yourself. It's a lesson in, well, in diplomacy. Have you any experience in that, Captain?" he asked.

Tanner nodded. "As a matter of fact, recently, yes, Sir, I do. But I also know that it's applied as needed, Sir. I take it that these," he said as he pointed to his lap, "are the most pressing ones?" he asked.

The admiral nodded. "That's a big 10-4, Captain. Handle them and then come back for more. See

Kelsey too for billeting quarters here on the landing port base. You'll be assigned a flyer of your own—careful though as they handle differently. We work here from oh nine hundred hours through to nineteen hundred hours—trying to get the job done. You can request through Kelsey anything you need. Oh—budget is not a problem at all anymore, it seems … just to get the damn four towers finished off and our Confederacy Council occupancy permits issued. In four months, Captain—that's all I've got for now," he said and sighed as he nodded his goodbyes and reached for one of those chiming tablets to his side.

Moments later, Tanner and Kelsey worked out his quarters, and Tanner received his paperwork for the flyer and IDs for his PDA so that he'd be networked into the academy communications systems.

"So, what's the scuttlebutt on when we do get the permits, Lieutenant?"

The Faraway alien cocked his head to one side—something Tanner noted his tail did at exactly the same time, which might be good to know in future—and half-smiled.

"Sir, local wagering has it at seven months at a minimum. Just saying, Sir," he said and smiled a bit.

Tanner nodded and smiled back as he picked up

the folders and tablets to leave. "'Bout where I'd put it—but let's see what we can do, shall we?" and he turned to leave the administration building and find his way over to the officer's residence to get his quarters squared away. Next would be the flyer yard to find his wheels—or wings—maybe and get over to the towers to see what he could see.

CHAPTER TWO

In the inner chamber of her apartment, the
Master Adept sat waiting. She had been doing just
that now for over an hour, and she was experienced
enough to know that some things could not be
rushed. She often looked at the far wall, wishing
she could see the lands around the Issian walled
city. Out there, she knew, life was hard, and yet she
knew what she would see if a window was there.

Seared plains and small foothills rimmed the city,
and beyond them lay more of the same for as far as
the eye could see. In fact, here on the southern
hemisphere, on the largest continent on Eons, those
hills ran more than four thousand miles running
east to west mostly but occasionally creating
canyons and even smaller buttes and mesas. For the
most part, no one lived from here to the western

sea; Dessau was the farthest city on the continent, and it lay among those hills too.

Scrub brush coated the hills but not a tree could be seen. The soil was so pitifully poor that such hardy vegetation could not grow. Some of the brush was brown, and still more was that parched orange rust color that came from scorched weather patterns that plagued the planet. For almost three generations, the ground had been able to support less and less vegetation, and crops had long since died. No matter what kind of fertilizers had been developed, the land could not grow enough food to support the people of Eons.

She knew Eons had not always been a desolate wasteland. Records going back ten centuries showed this had once been a fertile continent with abundant farms, prosperous cities, and a thriving agricultural commerce system..

For the last three centuries, the radiation from the blue sun over Eons had gradually changed the land. As the droughts increased, the soil and the economy dried up. Scientists predicted the young giant blue star would eventually find balance and agriculture would thrive again. Until then, the people of Eons were left to find other means to support themselves and their planet.

Having the academy here meant much for the Issians. It would change everything, more than most knew, for the Issians and their struggling economy.

She paused in her thinking as the first tremor of another mind entered her own consciousness, and she quickly let the falling feeling arise within her. Moments later, she was surrounded by others—not in person, but in the Issian mind grouping, which meant they could all see each other's minds and conference that way. This was the Issian Inner Council—the group that governed Eons.

She nodded to each but turned right away to the twins who had been invited to the mind group today.

"Zara and Ella, so good of you to join us, and while niceties are yes, nice, we all want to know what you've learned," she said in a hurry, trying to get to the point immediately.

Zara spoke up for the twins; she was the one who always took a leadership position, and while it was known that both twins were about equal in Issian potentials, Zara spoke for both. A woman of forty years of age, she and her identical twin, Ella, had been members of the most innermost group of Issians who helped to govern Eons—and their abilities too.

She was pretty in a sense, mature, with the hint of gray now in her hair. Like most Issians, she dressed in all black. Her top, leggings, and even her boots were black. She pushed back the edge of her hood so it lay out of the way on her shoulders, and her mind spoke up with a small degree of regret in her voice.

"Master and all here, I am afraid that we have little real news—but rumors do abound up on Aporia. While what we can report is factual, as I said, there are other items that we cannot as yet confirm," she said.

She looked at the few faces that were in the circle around her and shrugged.

"What we know is that Kendal Steyn is still working against us. She has been somewhat, um, successful in her recruitment of others to her cause—twins, of course. Her own twin, Mariam, is still being held in confinement in our MedWards and suffers as always. I will not go into what we—Ella and I—think caused that breakdown, but you all know how we feel. With Kendal actively working on the building of her own group of protesters, we think that this will become an issue that we will have to deal with soon. Deal with—we think—in a very formidable way," she said and then leaned back.

All present sat on that for a moment, and then all eyes turned to the Master Adept.

"Thank you, Zara, your abilities to provide us with evidence of this group is much appreciated. We, too, believe that if they get bigger and if they then decide to go public with their twisted reasonings, we will have to do something. One more thing—any visitors at the

MedWards for her twin?"

Zara shook her head. *"Not a single one for the past four months, Master. We have an inside source there and monitor same,"* she said.

The Master Adept nodded. *"So, for all here to consider, at the next mind grouping, we will need to discuss various methods to handle same. Remember, the protesters plan to gather converts, then publicize their beliefs to try to get us to stop our so far very successful Twin Selection program. We cannot allow that to happen. I want your own ideas on same at the next grouping …"* she said, and as she did the circle of other Adepts around her disappeared.

The Inner Council mind grouping was over.

She rose and left the inner chamber—what she often called her office, as if she needed one—and returned to the living area of her quarters in the tower that rose over the walled city.

Outside, she could still see the ruins of a farm just a few miles away, the barn leaning sickly and the farmhouse without a roof. Past that, the previously orderly corrals and paddock fences held a rail or two, but for the most part, they looked like they had been left to deteriorate for years. She knew the view a hundred miles or a thousand miles down the valley would be the same—long forsaken farms and buildings and the detritus of a once flourishing farming community … and that could be seen mile after mile.

We do what we do when it comes to twins, as we need to.

The ability to change a birth was one that only Issians with the most prolific of abilities could do.

Science said that monozygotic twins were formed after a blastocyst essentially collapsed, splitting the progenitor cells—those that contain the body's fundamental genetic material—in half, leaving the same genetic material divided in two on opposite sides of the embryo. And identical twins were formed.

But Issians had learned they could control the creation of twins by simply using their highly skilled minds to make the progenitor cells split into two, creating two embryos where there had been only one.

Of course, it only worked on females—male embryos resisted this kind of tampering remotely, and it always ended the embryo's life.

Females only. And seldom, but enough to help keep the Issians as adept as could be.

After all, the Master herself had once been a twin, as had all of the Inner Council …

#####

His flyer was blue, and it was the just a bit lighter than the blue of the background shield in the RIM

Navy icon of the dagger. It had two seats, with both having access to the center-mounted trackball controls. *Could carry,* Tanner thought, *at least a couple hundred pounds of cargo in the rear bay, but today it was just him.*

ID in—check. The flyer's AI flashed up a verified user notice on the dashboard display.

Power on—check. As Tanner hit the start button, the thrusters him mounted on each side behind him were up and running fine.

Belts on—check. He buckled his seatbelt and ensured it was secure.

Time to go, and he slowly used the trackball to lift off—up and up and then yaw to port—and then his thumb hit the throttles, and the flyer surged ahead.

Got some pep, he thought and grinned. *Wonder what this woulda been like with a load of Scotch on …*

Ahead, he could see the foothills, and he made his way toward them in a straight line.

No control towers and no flight plans either.

Eons was still a seat of your pants type of aeronautical system, he realized, *and that meant that biggest and fastest usually ruled.*

His gaze went down to the river below as he followed it upstream for a few miles until the canyon walls began to build around it. As those walls grew taller and taller, the four towers of the new academy came into view. They stood out, no doubt about that, for all to see. He knew that the administration tower, where he'd find his office, was in Tower Number Four, so he made his way there first.

Circling the tower, from top to bottom, he could see some still unfinished floors, some windows missing, a few welders perched what he'd call perilously on the scaffoldings, and yes, two floors just boarded up completely.

At ground level, he leveled off and took the flyer in for his first landing.

"Went well," he said to himself, as the flyer AI helped a bit, and he came to a stop only a hundred feet from the huge doorways and ramp up into the tower. He opened up the flyer canopy and hopped out—to be met right away by a Provost guard with a Merkel on his shoulder.

"Sir, ID, please," the guard asked, and Tanner nodded and beamed over the required docs from his wrist PDA.

The guard looked down at the display on his chest and nodded.

"Welcome, Captain Scott. Your offices, if that's where you're headed, are up on floor twenty-three. Right beside Rear Admiral Higgins' offices— you've no staff I think as yet though, Sir." The guard whirled around and went back to the small shack that was nearer the main doors.

Going to be pretty impressive when she's done, Tanner thought. There were enormous thirty-foot doorways with wood trim that was made from that wood from Anulet he'd so admired during the Duke's hunting party, but he couldn't remember the name of the wood. "Still, wonderful grain and colors," he said, as he walked in the now open double front doors.

Inside was a complete mess. Half-opened cartons of furniture were being manhandled onto dollies for inside deployment. Rows and rows of cases of pre-packed items—he had no idea what lay within—were being hand-bombed by what looked like students deeper within the lobby. Tech pieces, raw wires, ports, terminals, and monitors were all stacked up and waiting to go up in the elevators.

Elevators. He could see four of in the lobby, but three were sealed off with yellow tape and were not being used hence the holdup for all inward-bound goods and equipment.

He smiled to himself, went over to a man who appeared to be a senior tech, and interrupted him.

"Hi … can you tell me, please, why three of the elevators are not being used today?" Tanner said.

The tech raised his eyebrows. "Sir … Captain—sorry, yeah. Seems that these three are not allowed to be used as they've not been granted to do so by the RIM inspectors, Sir. You—like us—will learn to hate those guys too," he said, as he tried to balance one more monitor on the dolly in front of him and then helped to push it into the long, long line for the only working elevator.

Tanner grinned.

He went over to the closest sealed off elevator, tore down the yellow tape, kicked aside the signage that said NOT IN SERVICE, and then pressed his hand against the wall plate. The door opened. He went in, turned, and then hit the button for the next floor up, which happened to be floor four. The doors closed. The elevator went up to the fourth floor and the doors opened. He took a half step outside to look around, got back into the elevator, and pressed the button marked LOBBY. The elevator returned to the lobby floor.

He left the elevator and said quite loudly for all to hear, "I am Captain Scott. I have just made all the elevators fully functional. Use them as you will." He tore down the rest of the tape and kicked the signage out of his way.

All four elevators were now up and running.

"End of this one," he said to himself, and he watched as the lengthy line grew much shorter as workmen and dollies dived for those new elevators now in use.

One down, but thousands still left, he knew, and

he watched as the increase in functional elevators slowly began to chew down the traffic jam in the lobby.

He took the stairs, noting that cases had been left aside on some landing, but he got all the way up to the twenty-third floor and opened the door to same.

Here there was soft carpeting already laid, coved ceilings, and even art on the walls. Here, on what was the executive floor, he figured, everything was done, as this was where the academy administrators would be found. Registrars, CEOs, and principals, VIPs, deans, and other administrators would all be located here. Figures that it's ship-shape, he thought, as he walked across the soft carpet and down the long central corridor.

At a few doors that were open, he stuck his head in—beautiful new office furniture and wall units were already installed, and book cases and more art were on the walls. Looks like admin is ready … wonder how the student areas are, he thought, but in his gut, he knew there'd be a real difference.

He found a door with a large temporary sign that read Rear Admiral Higgins, and he looked in at an empty room.

And beside it was another office with sign that read Captain Scott. He went into his office and grinned.

Plain concrete floor.

A simple short desk with a folding chair.

No network hookups, no computer terminals, no communications or monitors—not a thing to work with.

Just a room and a seat.

He shook his head. No wonder the admiral worked out of the administration wing over at the landing port.

So will I, Tanner thought, and he smiled at how little he intended to be in his office.

Here is where the rubber meets the road as they used to say, so here at the towers is where I'll be.

He took the stairs down two at a time, and when he reached the lobby, he was met by the same senior tech he'd spoken to a half hour earlier.

"Sir, wanted to warn you—there's a couple of Provost guards and one of those damn RIM Building Inspectors looking for you," he said out of the corner of his mouth, and then he went back to slugging another big box in a pile of other boxes.

Tanner nodded, said, "Got it," and then turned to leave the tower lobby.

As he walked outside, he saw the guards around his flyer, and his jaw got a certain clench as he walked up to them.

"Can I help you, Provost?" he said to the lieutenant who stood in his way. Behind him, three more Provost guards were between them and the flyer. Beside the lieutenant, but a step or two back, stood some kind of a bureaucrat with too many folders and tablets in his hands.

"Sir, Provost Lieutenant Lismer. We have it on good report that you are the captain who is responsible for tearing down the elevator closed notices and signage and then letting workmen use same. Is that true, Captain—and a small note, Sir? That if that is true, then you may be charged with zoning infractions, Sir," he finished off.

His jaw still set, Tanner looked at the lieutenant.

"Lieutenant, might I ask if you recognize this uniform—my uniform?"

"Sir, yes, Sir—it's a Barony Navy captain's uniform, Sir."

"And Lieutenant, do you also know that the Barony is a Royal realm? One that is governed by our Baroness?"

The lieutenant nodded.

"And Lieutenant, are you also aware that as a Royal realm, we have our own laws and penalties for items that we determine are crimes?"

Again the lieutenant nodded, but a little slower.

"And are you aware, Lieutenant, that we also have beheadings in the Barony—that happen on the whim of our Baroness," Tanner said flatly, his voice edged like a guillotine.

The lieutenant did not nod. He did not move, as

he seemed to be processing what he'd just heard.

"And as the 2IC here on Eons for the new academy build—only the rear admiral can tell me what to do—I also have the ear of the Baroness. What would you like me to do when I find something that I can fix—fix it, or perhaps just pass along the culprits to my Baroness? Your choice, Lieutenant," Tanner said with intensity.

The lieutenant started to half-turn to the bureaucrat but stopped when he saw the man had taken several steps backward. He turned back to face Tanner as he found himself alone.

"Sir, fix things, of course. Just like you did today, Sir. Job well done, Sir," he said quickly, snapped a salute, said "With me," and marched away followed by his other Provost guards.

Tanner, however, held out a hand to stop the bureaucrat.

"Just so you know—your bullshit ends today. I want all inspections done same day as you get notifications that tasks are completed—and passed too. Otherwise, I'll just add a name-your name—to the Baroness's list. Got me?" he said, his eyes drilling down into the poor man's face

That got him a nod, several nods, and the bureaucrat almost ran away toward the tower.

Tanner got back into his flyer and began the startup routine.

Tower Four done, now on to tower Three.
He wondered what he'd find there.

#####

In Aporia, in the far west dome, Kendal sat and
stared out the side windows toward the small
garden that she'd so carefully tended the past few
years. Once it held roses; her fame for being able to
even get them to root in such low gravity here on
the Eons moon was a mainstay of her reputation
within the local gardening community. She had
used a simple trick her mother had shown her
decades before—tying the roots down to sections of
plastic pipe filled with sponges. That kept the roots
mired deeper than they'd actually grow, and the
sponges allowed more water to collect there as well.
Her roses grew and that was a nice thing.

Now, they lay dying in the ruined garden. The
petals of what had blossomed earlier had fallen off
the blooms, and the usually thick and thorny stems
were brown and sagging. It had been months since
she'd even been out to tend to her garden, and she
felt no shame in her lack of attention to things that
grew.

She also realized she'd been paying almost no
attention to David either—and that was unlike her
normally. Since he'd lived with her for more than a
dozen years, she'd always been the aunt who cared.

When her sister had died years ago, David had come to her as a shy introverted pre-teenager, and he'd grown to be a shy introverted twenty-three-year-old man. A techie guru, he'd just quit his job with the Academy Network IT department after working there for only two years, and yet running a department all on his own hadn't seemed to matter to him. Now, he kept pretty much to himself in his room out back; and other than being on the net all the time, he had little to say to her as usual. If she had had any other way than to get him to help her with her Mariam issues, she would have used those avenues. But as she'd hesitantly explained what she wanted him to do—hack the MedWards network— he had just nodded and held up a hand, she remembered.

"Not a problem, Auntie. Been in already a while back—nothing there really but patient records, vids of procedures, and the like. What are you after?" he had asked, and that had stopped her cold.

She'd then taken more than an hour to explain to him who his grandmother had been; what the inner circle was; and how twins were a new but necessary way for them to solidify their future. And about the aunt he'd never met—Mariam.

He'd been a bit shocked—not that his life experience would have ever helped him to get ready for this kind of truth. He nodded. He said

51

he'd have the vids on tape by dinner, and she'd spent the longest afternoon ever at her storefront wondering if he could provide that vid—and he had.

She'd asked him if he'd watched it all—and he nodded and looked away from her face to speak.

"Auntie, she is your twin that I can see—anyone can see. But she looks like she's in pain and mad and frustrated—yet if they keep her in the secure wards, she must be a threat to herself. Right?" he asked, and she knew he wanted to feel that this was true.

It was not.

But she had no real reason to tell him the whole truth, so she just nodded.

He handed her the thumb drive and left the kitchen to go back to his room.

She didn't see him for days after that, and when he finally came to the supper table, the topic of Mariam was never mentioned again.

Like my garden, and she half-smiled to herself.

As if things that I tend grew at all, only to die when nature said it was their time.

"Just wish that we humans were like that," she said, her voice spitting venom against the window.

Worried she might be late, she stopped her reverie out the window. She had to get going.

Minutes later, she bustled down the alley in front

of her small bungalow in the west dome, headed
toward the bus, and boarded it less than five
minutes later. She knew she'd still be late, but not
too late, and she thought about what she was going
to say and how much malice to include. New twins
meant new to more than the group. New twins
meant unknowing twins.

She wished she could have avoided what came
next, but the warnings were always less than a
minute in coming.

Her gut seized up like a cramp from hell. Her
head ached instantly, and the pounding in her
temples could be seen as she grasped the top of the
bus seat in front of her and breathed slowly in and
out, in and out.

She knew what the seizure was—it was her twin,
Mariam, crying out for help. Mariam reached out to
her twin with her brain on full throttle as she
screamed in her locked MedWard room miles away
from the bus. She did this almost daily trying to
reach out to find her sister, her twin, to ask for her
help, and all Kendal could do was to breathe in and
out, in and out.

She hadn't been able to visit her in person now in
months as the pain of seeing what Mariam had
become was so traumatic.

Now her eyes welled up with tears, and her
breathing was ragged but still the same in and out

pattern. One of her legs was now twisted beneath her, but she knew it would pass.

Across from her and up a seat, a youngster stared at her, wondering what was wrong, and Kendal just held up a hand and forced out the words "Got a cramp ..." and that seemed to work as the teenager turned back to look out the window.

As Mariam was given a larger dose of whatever it was they used on her, her reaching out started to ebb, and Kendal was able to straighten out her leg, loosen her grip on the seat, and sit up a bit straighter. The cramps were leaving as her stomach returned to normal, and the throbbing in her temples began to subside too.

"They'd pay for this. The Issian inner circle would pay for this dearly," she said to herself repeatedly as her stop came up at the edge of the downtown section of the center dome.

As she left the bus, she nodded to the teenager and half-smiled. A few minutes later, she found herself at the front door of a small commercial building with a large sign painted on the glass storefront that read Twins Cooperative and in she went.

Her assistant bustled over immediately, and Kendal could see that already there were four new groups of twins sitting in the larger room off to the side waiting for the meeting to start.

"Hi, Kendal," her assistant, Jane, said and stuffed some files into her hand. She leaned back and then took a good look at her. "Did you have another of those ... those incidents?" she questioned as she squeezed Kendal's arm.

Kendal nodded, handed Jane her coat, grabbed the files, and went in to sit and lead the new twins meeting.

She made her introductions. She listened to each of the twins as they introduced themselves individually and then went on to point out why they were here and what they might be looking for from such a group.

One of them said she had seen some of the Twins Cooperative members protesting at a recent public inner circle presentation and she wondered why. She and her twin had come to find out.

Kendal nodded. *Here we go.*

"It's often that we protest, because some twins — not all twins, but those of us who have been used by the inner circle, know that their meddling has cost lives. Many lives — and while I'm sure some of you doubt what I'm saying, let me just ask you this," she said.

"It is true that twins share — as I'm sure you all agree here — some kind of a special bond that others — non-twins — do not know about at all. Do we agree there?" she asked and everyone nodded.

"It is also true—and I'm no doctor, but we have the full medical reports on file, which, yes, you can see—that at the time of conception, it is possible using standard medical procedures to create twins. Monozygotic twins may also be created artificially by embryo splitting. It can be used as an expansion of IVF to increase the number of available embryos for embryo transfer, which was discovered more than hundreds of years ago. So medicine can create twins, do you agree here too?"

Everyone in the room nodded again. This was not new and had been reported in the news often.

"One more thing then that you need to know. Each of the current—and from what we can determine the past as well—members of the Inner Council from our Master Adept on down is a twin."

Not a head nodded. Some faces looked like they wanted to ask a question, but Kendal held up a hand.

"Wait—I know. You've seen the current Inner Council, and you've never been told or had any idea that they were twins, right?"

Again, everyone nodded.

"Because the twin—the ones we've never seen—did not live. They all were stillborn. Every single one of them. And do you know why?

Nodding once more meant that she was making

her point.

"Because instead of using medical procedures to split the embryo—the Inner Circle used their minds to do that splitting and transferred over from one of the twins all the chlorians and genes to the other. That made the resulting live born twin superior— and the stillborn one really just an empty shell. The medical reports spell all this out—but what you need to know is that there is a systematic program carried out by the Inner Council to use twins to gain and hold their positions," she said quietly and looked around the room.

Two of the twins stared at her. Their faces were questioning which meant her points had been made with these two.

Two more had leaned back and were half-smiling. They'd never be back.

And the remaining two sets of twins were shaking their heads—they'd need to read the reports, and she called out to Jane to bring in the coffee and tea and those damn heavy binders.

Each took a refreshment and then looked over the binders and cherry picked at what they'd read.

One of the won't-be-backs spoke up. "Ma'am, what you said—is there any truth to this? I mean, truth that doesn't come in a ten-pound three-ring binder?"

Kendal nodded. It usually came down to this too.

She eyed Jane and nodded. On the near wall, the large view-screen lit up, and the inside of the MedWard room of a patient, who was tied down—restrained they called it—to her bed filled the screen.

She was facing the other way from the camera, but her tangled hair was knotted and very unkempt. Her bare skinny legs jutted out from below the gown. Her leg hair was long, and her toenails were long, curled, and a dull yellow. She was tossing one arm trying to get it loose, but the tie-downs were solid, and she failed again and again.

As her head thrashed, the camera showed she had an open sore on the close temple. Pus caked it and dried up blood surrounded it.

And then she turned her head over to face the camera.

And it was Kendal's face.

Ragged and ravaged and ugly, but it was Kendal's face.

The gasp from the room of new twins was loud and very audible.

"That is my twin—Mariam. Our mother was Master Colleen, one of the Inner Council more than forty years ago. She was pregnant and the Inner Council tried to take her embryo and make twins. They succeeded and yes, I'm the one who got her sister's share of all things that make one human. But instead of being stillborn, Mariam was born as you see her now. There but not there. Alive but not alive, and a prisoner in the MedWard for those decades now," she said flatly.

She sipped her water.

"So yes, we do have proof. And yes, we want something done about this too. We want the practice of creating new Inner Council members using twins and this mental procedure to stop. Stop now. Stop today. So yes, we protest even though we know that none—or rather so very few—even listen to us. Or believe us."

The new twins were all quiet. The two who Kendal had figured would leave to never return were still sitting too, perhaps ...

She went on to close the meeting.

"We know you've just been asked to digest a lot of new information. We know that twins are the only ones who get this too. We know that you need time. Our next regularly scheduled meeting for all our members is next week at eighteen hundred hours. Please just let Jane know if you intend to come so we can schedule refreshments. I thank you all for coming to learn ..."

Minutes later, Jane looked at her and held up a hand palm up.

"Don't know—might be all of them," Kendal

said, meaning that perhaps all four sets of twins would be back.

Jane nodded and then patted her on the shoulder. "We need to talk about budgets for the big academy opening and how we want to disrupt that sometime today," she said as she began to clean up the empty cups and snacks.

Kendal grabbed a pastry and balanced it on her file folders as she went out of the large communal space to go to her office.

More to plan. More to fund. Being a twin was twice as much work as anyone had ever imagined.

#####

Tanner reminded himself that a soft Faraway alien's tail that would simply drop to the floor and lie still with little twitches meant that the owner was going to be approachable and work with him. At least that's what it seemed like.

Again, he was sitting in the anteroom to the admiral's offices, and again he was waiting for some time. From the large windows on the side wall, the bright sunlight streamed inside, and one could feel the heat even here in the air-conditioned offices. Outside, if he squinted just a little, Tanner could see ships that were in port, getting serviced or delivering goods perhaps. There was an Alex'n sphere ship—a larger one than he'd seen before—

close by, and the ship's chandlers had steady
streams of delivery trucks lined up at her cargo
ports. Beside her, but a bit to port, lay two frigates
—from the Duchy, it appeared, and Tanner
wondered what they were doing as they seemed to
be buttoned up and ready to depart—or maybe
they'd just arrived.

Well past them, almost at the far edge of the
enormous landing port tarmac sat a Barony Navy
ship, and Tanner saw that it was the frigate *Callisto*
with the twin crowns shining in the bluish sunlight.
Tanner knew there had been a group of interns
being sent to Eons for their inclusion in the new
academy, so he assumed that the *Callisto* had been
the carrier of same. Wonder whom they brought
and just how much help a hundred or so cadets
would be—but then any help at all seems like a
good idea. With the huge move-ins of equipment
and desks and the like, bodies with hands were a
good idea.

He glanced once again at Lieutenant CoSharan,
the admiral's assistant, who was busy on his
console was and was either too busy to
acknowledge him or just wanted to look too busy.
His tail was just lying on the floor though, which
made Tanner think about the engineers who
designed office chairs for all the aliens that lived
here on the RIM. Faraway aliens had tails, Ttseens

needed boosters, and DenKoss fish needed—well, they needed a tank really. He shook his head. *Beyond me.*

He contemplated tuning his PDA into the latest newscast, but then he remembered that news had been taken over by celebrity news—and how badly did he need to know about the breakup of yet another unknown vid star. He shook his head again.

The summons to appear here this morning was not surprising—he wondered *how much of a dressing down he'd be given in that he'd circumvented all the building codes and bylaws just to get those three extra elevators up and running.*

The door to the admiral's inner offices burst open, and he came out in a hurry with a stack of files tucked under one arm.

Dropping off those files in a pile on the credenza behind his assistant, he quickly marched right over to Tanner.

And grinned.

"So ... they behead folks over in the Barony, do they?" he said as he clapped Tanner on the shoulder.

"Glad to see you found a way to get one of our issues fixed. Heard back about it big time though from everyone from bylaw control to head of the Provost Guard, from Customs whose excise tax is now unpaid—the list is long. But, the elevators are running. Well done, lad. More of same—much more, I'm afraid, lies ahead. Oh—and Gallipedia reports that it's been two hundred years since anyone was beheaded in the Barony—treason, I think, was the crime. But nice one, Captain!" he said, as he shook his head and went back to his own office.

Lieutenant CoSharan cleared his throat, and when he had Tanner's attention, he waved him over with a file in hand.

"Captain—you'll need to shepherd the latest batch of student cadets over to quarters—they just came in on the *Callisto*. Find CPO Pope over at the quartermaster's office, get the cadets checked in and issued billet items, and then march them over to— let's see"—the lieutenant looked down at his monitor—"they're going to be in Officers' Building C-3. Get them squared away, appoint someone in the group to be their cadet leader, and then have him—or her—report back here to me STAT. We'll arrange for transport over to the new academy site for them then. Got that, Captain?" the alien said, and for a moment, Tanner felt like a cadet himself.

But he nodded, took the file, and then left the administration building to traipse over to the *Callisto* and pick up his newest helpers—*if one could call any cadets that.*

#####

David knew he'd have little time, but if his plan worked, he'd be able to handle the task easily.

He'd walked his block, using an anonymous WiFi finder, and had located the target house only a dozen feet down the block from his Aunt Kendal's home. The WiFi that this house was using was fine, right up to date, but the router that was in use was an older model. Like many net users, what worked was what you keep, so when these people moved in they simply brought their old router and plugged it in. He'd checked on the public database, and they'd lived there almost five years,you were you're doing.

He eyed some of the blue boxes that folks had brought out to the curb to get their recyclables picked up tomorrow morning and remembered he had to still do that back at Aunt Kendal's house.

He smiled as he slowly walked the length of the block and crossed the next street. At the third house on his right, he stopped to turn to his left to look out of the dome. Craters and more craters made their way toward the horizon. There was a vast plain there too, and he could still see the remaining vertical struts of the large signs that had held advertisements. Someone who was a smart marketing guy had figured if you pointed a sign with the name of your product at the dome, folks couldn't help but read it, increasing brand exposure and resulting revenues too.

That really got under the skin of the city council back then—what, seventy years ago he thought—*and they'd quickly outlawed all advertising outside the dome. So the signs had come down, yet the old steel I-bars still climbed up hundreds of feet but now held nothing. No advertisements, not a single one.*

David nodded. *That was how it should be—smart council back then—*unlike what he'd heard Aunt Kendal ranting about to her staff when she worked from home sometimes. She said she'd find a way to show them what was right under their noses and get even with the Inner Circle.

This time, David grunted. Politics. *He reminded himself he wanted none of it.*

As he moved a few feet to his right, pretending to be looking for the perfect picture, he brought up the large camera to his face and sighted ... moved farther right ... sighted ... back left a step and then took a few real photos.

Part one, done ... as his peers online had said over and over, a large part of a hack—any hack—done in person was to ensure you looked like you belonged. Like you had done this hundreds of times and you were really just part of the background.

He looked down at his camera. It was out of real film, and he looked around where he was. Not surprisingly, as he'd planned this a month ago, he was just a few feet from a large square masonry planter, about three feet square, holding some kind of flower at the front edge of the house's lawn. But more importantly, the edge of the box was six inches thick. Thick enough for him to balance his camera on which he did and then pulled the bag over his head to get more film.

The house was quiet—he'd planned for this to happen mid-afternoon, and so far, he had not seen another person on the street.

He rummaged around in the bag, finding the holster of a roll of new film, and he placed it on the edge of the planter too.

The bag he also placed on the planter, but he made sure to have one-half or so lean over the dirt at the edge of the planter's box. Part two, done ... get all your ducks in a row—a perfect row, he knew.

He dusted off his hands—they'd yelled at him that a real photographer would have used some kind of aerosol spray to get any and all dust and particles off, but he'd nixed that idea. "Just an amateur," he said to himself, as he slowly unlatched the back end of the big camera.

He pulled down on the red toggle inside at the

rear, and then with both hands, he squeezed the twin releases and the film holster dropped into his hands. He carefully moved it to the edge of the planter box and balanced it on the masonry.

He inserted the new film holster canister—

"Hey, whatcha doing?" a voice said from his left.

Next door to the house with the planter, some man had come out with what looked like a full box of recyclables, and he'd stopped down his driveway, eying David.

David grinned, remembering that smiles make all sorts of questions diminish.

"Hey, just reloading my big camera—I just needed somewhere to place it so it'd not get any dirt or dust—just using the planter box—that's okay, right?" he asked, making sure his voice was polite and respectful.

The man grunted and then began to tote his blue box out to the curb. In moments, he had deposited it there and had returned to his own house.

David smiled, hooked up the new film holster, and snapped the camera shut.

"And now, the crux of the whole matter," he said to himself.

He twisted a bit to his right, picked up the used film holster, and slowly wedged it into his bag, or at least that's what it looked like to anyone else. But in fact, his right hand was already deep in the bag, opening the false bottom, and using his hand like a trowel, he was moving dirt out of his way. He had to go down at least a foot, but the planter had been watered earlier, and the soil was easy to dig into. At the foot mark or so he thought, he pulled the used film holster back up with his left hand turning it ninety degrees for a better fit, and then he began to push it back down.

His right hand, however, grabbed his repeater, in its watertight container, and he dropped it into that new foot-deep hole and quickly covered it up with the soil he'd just removed. Tapping it down and closing the false bottom, he stood up off his knees to push down on the top of the used film holster once more. Then he grabbed the sides of the bag itself and jerked them up and down a couple of times to seat the holster and put the bag back on his shoulder.

Picking up his camera, he clicked the load button and then the auto AI button, and the display screen on the back flashed him the ready icon.

New film, check.

Repeater in place, check.

Anonymous WiFi coming up, check.

He grinned at the craters and the big plain and smiled.

He even took a couple more shots from that point too.

And then he went home to find that his repeater was working as it infiltrated that house's older router, and he was now on the net but pretending to be living at that house. For a moment, he felt a bit guilty, but then he remembered his peers had said that if you can't even protect your own WiFi, you don't deserve to even be on the net.

"Works for me," David said.

CHAPTER THREE

Flying into Tower Number Three was a hoot, Tanner thought, as he got to do a big swirly turn off to port to come around and then up the cliff face of the canyon to land quickly at the tower landing pad. "Lots of other flyers here already," he said to himself, and he could see that most did not carry the same blue coloration and RIM Confederacy Navy insignia either, though there were a few of same.

He jumped out, nodded to the Provost guard at the small hut at the edge of the tarmac, and walked slowly toward the massive double doors. He had to remember to ask what kind of wood that was, but he filed that away for later as a man in civvies was coming up to him with some degree of haste.

"Sir—uh—Captain, is it? Sir, can I get some help

here?" the man said and thrust a wad of unruly documents into Tanner's hands. Who the man was and what the issue was were forgotten or he just neglected to say.

But Tanner had to at least somewhat follow procedures.

"Yes, it's Captain Scott. And you are?" he asked nicely, not even looking at the papers yet.

"Well, if you construction types learned to read and to follow academy procedures, you'd see that I am Professor Nigel Watkins, the academy ethics teacher, and I'm about fed up with the slowness of all of this. And now, I find that my textbooks—two of which I wrote myself—cannot be here in time for the upcoming semester. And I find that to be someone else's fault—hardly my own," he said, his voice whining out the words.

Tanner nodded and looked down at the papers. As he leafed through them, he noted that the textbook publisher claimed there was not enough time—four months, mind you, Tanner thought—to get the textbooks printed, bound, and then shipped to Eons.

He looked at the upset professor with a raised eyebrow. "Professor Watkins—it seems this issue is not with us—the construction crew—at all but with your own publisher," Tanner said dryly.

The professor nodded but then shook his head

71

back and forth. "Yes—the publisher can't fulfill the orders because of the stupid construction taking so much longer, and that has backed up all textbook orders with them. I hear that there's hundreds of these same textbook issues. What are you going to do about it, Captain?" he said.

Upset? Yes, the professor was upset, and at this point, Tanner had no idea as to why this textbook issue had arisen at all.

"Professor, Tower Number Three is the Quartermasters and Services Tower—and this is my first visit to same. Let me look into this, will you, and I'll make it a point to get back to you. Today," he said, and he wondered how he could do that, but he smiled anyway.

The professor nodded and then reminded Tanner that he now had a name of a person whom he'd call for updates on this issue and more importantly, he stated flatly, a name he would assign blame to at the next full faculty meeting with the admiral in a few hours as that next meeting was today. And as a reminder to the captain, he shared that as the president of the Union Local, he would also have sway over the professors as a whole too.

Tanner nodded, gave back the untidy pile of documents, and finally made his way into Tower Number Three. Like the administration tower he'd been in yesterday, the lobby was huge and soaring, full at this point with workmen and movers, using all four elevators, he noted, to move goods and equipment up and into the tower.

"Morning, Corporal," Tanner said to one of the marines standing on what looked like picket duty at the side of the lobby rotunda. "Mind telling me about the layout of the tower?" he asked.

"Sir, yes, Sir. Lobby is here—well, you can see that. Far doors lead to admin offices for the academy quartermaster, Provost guard offices, that sort of thing. Elevator up to the fourth floor, and the academy library takes up that whole floor, Sir. That's where most of those equipment cases are heading," he said, as he pointed to a long grouping of wooden cases on dollies.

"Library takes up from floor four up to nine; quartermaster services and such up to floor thirty-one, and the balance of the fifty-two floor tower is— well, I've no idea, Sir. Only been up to thirty-one myself, Sir," he said, and Tanner got the gist of the layouts.

He nodded, thanked the Provost corporal, and then went over to one of the elevators that seemed to have more people than equipment lined up. Moments later, he got off on floor four—the library entrance.

He had to pick his way around more wooden cases, equipment technicians, and packaging supplies that were now being tossed into piles to be taken away as waste. He slowly worked his way into the vast open space that would one day be a library.

"But not today," he said to himself, as workmen were still assembling shelving units by the dozens as others laid out the built ones according to some kind of design layouts they had. He smiled. *If there was one thing he remembered from his own Earldom Academy days and their library, there was always somewhere to goof off—sleep even. Or more and that brought him a real smile.*

He wandered. He looked at the expansive windows along the canyon side of the tower and was glad he didn't suffer from a fear of heights. He walked along that complete wall and was stopped near the end by a techie.

"Sir, careful along the rest of this wall. We're running big power cables up to this exact spot—for the POD printers—and we don't want anyone to bump into a live feed. Not to worry—all is supposed to be dead lines 'til later—but one just never knows in new construction, Sir," he said and turned away.

Tanner asked, "Can you tell me—what does POD mean?"

The techie nodded as he was stripping cables of their protective plastic collars. "Sir, that means print on demand—you know, where you can simply supply something as an electronic doc at one end of the printer and the book comes out the other."

He stripped more of the plastic using some kind of specialized pliers, and Tanner said "Bingo," to himself.

As he moved through the library, he eventually found the administration offices and popped his head inside to see if he could—

"Can I help you, Captain?" a voice said from behind a monitor at a desk in the corner.

He ambled over and smiled down at the young woman who was eating a kind of lunch—if you could call a salad a lunch.

"Yes, I was just wondering if you could tell me—is there a time line for the completion of the library as a whole? All up and books on shelves, printers ready—is there a date for that?" he asked.

She nodded as she tucked the edge of a piece of something green into the corner of her mouth and then grinned back at him. "Word is we'll be up before much else is—say in about two months or so. But the classrooms over in Tower Number Two are the slowpokes, Sir. Why?" she asked, as she chewed on her healthy lunch.

He smiled and said, "No reason ... just wanted to know," and he left her to get more healthy.

He went and did a complete walk on the other side of the library too, the non-canyon side, and it too was being finished. There were several workers here, all busy. All engaged. All were actually working, which made him think the two-month time line was a doable one.

Walking out the library doors, he remembered the Provost corporal had said that the quartermasters administration offices were both down in the lobby itself as well as taking up from floor nine to thirty-one. He waited for the next elevator and then went up ten floors to floor fourteen. He got off amid a huge pile of packaging cartons, boxes, and cases, all being slowly tossed into disposal units by a couple of cadets. He nodded to them and noted they sped up considerably as they recognized his captain's rank.

He entered a set of double doors again and noted there was a security screen protecting the rest of the floor from entry by unauthorized visitors. The screen was unfinished so he just walked through and around the first tall stack of crates, and then he was challenged.

"Sir, sorry—this is a restricted quartermaster staff only area. You will need to leave immediately," the Provost sergeant said as he blocked Tanner's path.

Tanner nodded.

Quite right. Properly handled and with the right

degree of politeness, yet the velvet glove did have an iron fist within, and he noted the Merkel on the guard's shoulder.

"Sorry, Sergeant, just walking around. My apologies, I'll leave and go back down to the lobby administration offices.

The sergeant nodded but held firm in his stance and made sure to take a couple of steps forward to ensure that Tanner pressed the DOWN button on the elevator and then continued to watch him leave the floor.

Down in the lobby, Tanner moved past the large lines of crates and over to the quartermaster's offices. Inside at the long counter, a young alien from Ttseen presented himself and said, "May I help you, Captain?"

Tanner nodded and asked if he could provide the location and time of the upcoming faculty meeting, and the Ttseen told him they were weekly meetings held over in Tower Number Four on floor sixteen.

He nodded, realizing he could swing by there in a little while and make that meeting without any problem.

He spent the next hour walking other floors of Tower Number Three—not the quartermaster floors but above them in the thirty-first floor.

Empty. Not a single divider or office or room laid out at all. The elevator doors opened on an empty space. Enormous windows on the canyon side looked out at Eons and on the other side down to the tarmac or to Dessau in the distance.

But that was it.

Expansion, Tanner thought. *Maybe this is for the Academy getting bigger, but surely, the costs would have been quite large for this kind of future planning to occur.*

He shook his head. He was a starship captain—a navy man, not an urban planner. "But sure seemed to be an expensive way to build," he said as he took the elevator all the way down to the lobby and then went out to his flyer.

Five minutes later, he landed over on the other side of the canyon at Tower Number Four, the administration tower, and was able to just crowd into an elevator as it was going up. He helped the three cadets manhandle the top-heavy dolly out of the elevator car and then pressed the button for floor sixteen and got off to be met by a Provost guard who gave him the once over.

"Sir—help you?" he offered very politely.

"Yes, I'm looking for the faculty meeting? Can you direct me?" Tanner said just as politely.

He was sure the guard had more questions, but he turned and pointed down a long corridor off to the right.

"Yes, Sir. Take this hallway down about halfway, then take a left, and the big conference room is off to your left a few more yards down that side corridor."

As Tanner walked, he once again noted the beautiful surroundings on the floor. *Art on the walls. A few small seating areas spaced down the long corridor too,* and as he met the side corridor, he turned to his left.

Ahead behind a solid glass wall, he could see more than fifty people in civvies sitting around a huge table, while at one end, the admiral sat alone. As he entered the room, the admiral looked up, smiled, and patted the table beside him to indicate that Tanner should come and sit there. And he did.

"Meetings are boring and are supposed to be boring," he said to himself as the admiral opened up the meeting soon after that. Tanner nodded as he was introduced as the 2IC for the new academy facility building and half-smiled back at the more than fifty unsmiling faces.

The admiral was going over the various timelines; issues that had held them up were named and labeled, and workarounds were identified. Mostly the issues were with the facilities here being ready to be equipped and built-ins being done. "Sometimes," Higgins added, "the suppliers were behind, and that made everything else get out of whack too."

Tanner nodded when he should have and looked

interested when he should have. He wished to be anywhere on a bridge rather than sitting and listening to this. His mind drifted to the Lady St. August for a moment, but he shoved that away as soon as he thought of her, and it worked or so it seemed.

"Captain, sorry?" the admiral interrupted his train of thought and looked over at him.

"Sir?" Tanner said.

"I meant, did you have anything else to add? You've only been here a couple of days, but you must by now have something to say to our faculty," he said, as he gathered up some of the papers in front of him.

Tanner thought and then spoke up.

"One thing I did learn today was that some of you—perhaps many of you—may be facing some issues with textbook deliveries in time for our first semester," he said and that got quite a few nods from the assembled faculty.

"I also learned, that in our Library, we are going to have full POD capabilities to be up and running in about two months, which is well before the start of that semester. Seems to me that all a prof might have to do is to deliver to the library electronic copies of their textbooks. The library can print same and then put them in the hands of the first semester students," he said and then held up his hand to stop some of the faculty from interrupting him as a few were starting to rise in their seats.

"Yes, I know about copyright. Yes, I know about costs. Yes, I know even that some of you are the authors of those books and there might be royalties involved. But my job is to get the first semester at our new RIM Navy Academy up and running. You may have an alternate workaround—but that one will work for you. Plus, as a sidebar, it would make your publishers more eager to provide the texts if they learn that they'd lose revenues if we do it our way," he said, and that got a few nods from the crowd.

The admiral chimed in. "That's what we'll do. POD if they can't meet our deadlines. Plus I'll ensure that there will be small student costs too so that the books will be produced and used. End of discussion, and the end of our meeting. See you all in one week," he said, and he gathered up all of his items and turned to Tanner.

"Nice catch on that, Captain. I take it you've not as yet been over to Tower Number Two yet? And your offices are ready for you beside my own down in admin at the Dessau landing port," the admiral said and bustled out.

A hand touched Tanner's arm and he turned to face Professor Watkins.

"Captain—thank you. That will get my students

the texts they need. I had no idea that speaking to you a few hours ago would get me an answer that I can work with so quickly. My thanks—my students thank you too, Captain," he said, and he reached out to shake Tanner's hand.

"You have at least one friend on the faculty, Captain—come to find me anytime you've issues," he offered and smiled.

Tanner nodded and then remembering that he was going to be a faculty member himself in four months, he smiled too.

#####

She spun on her heel and strode down the alley between the treadmills, aiming at the farthest one from the group of other early morning gym users behind her. When she reached that last machine, she noted it had an Out of Order notice taped to the display plate. She threw her metal water bottle against the close wall that was currently showing some kind of scene from some other world than Neres, and the screen skipped the vid and went black.

Angry?

"Yes," she said to herself, *I am about as angry with Tanner as I've ever been.*" She was even angrier than she was when he'd drunkenly stolen a robo-cab out of her Embassy lineup years ago on Conclusion and had been too drunk to even acknowledge his failure at protocol days later.

Upset?

"*Yes, I am upset,*" she said to herself, as she sat on the edge of a close-by treadmill and hung her head over the top of her crossed arms. In her now sweaty gym outfit, with the tight leggings and bodice, she was one large sweat-ball, but she knew that not going to the gym every other day meant she was going to fall into that fat Royal group that she so didn't want to join. She pulled the towel down from around her left shoulder, mopped her face and the back of her neck, and dragged a towel end down between her breasts as she tried to get the sweat off of her.

"*More sweat coming,*" she said to herself, as she rose, dropped the towel on the floor beside the treadmill she was at, and said, "Go" to the AI that ran that gym machine.

As it started up, she half-smiled. *Why couldn't she fall in love with an AI type of guy—one who'd do as ordered all the time and comply? To her wants and needs all the time. Yes, that was the kind of man that she'd thought Tanner might have been—except, as she shook her head and began to quicken her pace, not really.*

The kind of man that Tanner was, was a navy man. A follow-the-rules type except when the rules held you back. An obey-the-rules type except when

you had to stray outside same. She remembered
that he'd saved her life—along with other heads of
state too—at the prison riots on Halberd. She
remembered he'd been drunk or half-drunk most of
his life here on the RIM. She remembered he'd
beaten the Pirates too, as well as making his own
vacuum jump to save the Ikarian vaccine from
being stolen on the Barony Hospital Ship.

*All in all, exactly the right type of man to be a
Baroness's husband—not that she was the Baroness as
yet. But one day soon.*

She picked up the pace again. The treadmill
gauged her increase in her pace, and the machine
sped up to a full nine miles an hour, her normal
pace for the next fifteen minutes.

Tanner had left her.

*Or, perhaps even more honestly, he had asked her to
abdicate' her position as a Royal in the Barony—the heir
apparent, in fact, to rule someday. To give that up.*

She'd never give up the Barony.

He had said that he felt like he was just the same
as the furniture. That even though he loved her—it
was the Royal in her that he couldn't handle.

And then she threw him out of her bedroom, off
the Sterling, and with the prompting from Gillian,
her Adept Issian, he was assigned to Eons as
punishment. *He could help order new blackboards for
all she cared.* She pounded down even harder, and

the treadmill AI upped the pace to eleven miles an hour.

Sweat came, of course, and she let it run down her brow and even enjoyed the slight sting as the salty fluid filled up an eye. She drove her legs even more, her pace increasing once again, and she knew she was up there with her own personal best as the treadmill AI chimed again, and she hit a full twelve miles an hour.

She ran.

She hated him.

She ran.

She loved him.

She almost fell when that broke into her train of thought, and the machine slowed instantly.

Gillian the Adept had said — or at least implied — that the punishment tour of duty for Tanner was an idea from the Master Adept herself. Or did she? It had been broached by Gillian. She went along with it, but now she wondered what else might be behind that duty, and she nodded as she reached forward and toggled the treadmill to begin the slowdowns.

As she slowed her gait, the whole thing was sounding somewhat odd to her.

Why in the world would a pirate-defeating, prison-riot-defeating navy captain be needed to count blackboards?

Why indeed.

She slowed and stopped as the treadmill chimed at her, and she stepped down to sit on the edge once again, picking up the towel to sop up what she could.

Probably lost like five pounds so far. Rowing machine will be the end of today though.

But Tanner—she missed him.

She missed that slightly crooked smile and the crinkle of the crow's feet at the side of those light blue eyes.

She missed him.

She grunted, rose, and went back up the aisle toward the side off to the right where the rowing machines were in a row and wondered what time it was.

She looked up at the ceiling—she didn't know why she always did that—to ask the Sterling AI what the shipboard time was and found it was coming up to lunchtime.

She also wondered *how long in days it might take for the frigate to get to Eons,* but she left that unasked as yet.

More thought here, and if possible, maybe even a small heart-to-heart with her Gillian might be the first thing to do.

#####

"Dr. Twelves ... please report to MedWards Maternity dome, room number three-one-one-two, please," the AI said throughout the MedWard domes, and as he heard his name again, Dr. Twelves nodded. Doctors were always called last, when all the other staff and patient were ready and waiting. So it was time.

Finishing up his quick lunch—*if one could call some kind of cardboard wrapped around wilted veggies and then deep fried so it'd be cooked, lunch*—he jammed the tail end of the stuffed tortilla into his mouth and dusted off his hands.

We should have more napkins; the food should be better too; and more importantly, maybe we could eat out in the major public areas of the Aporia dome city— instead of being locked up here in the MedWard domes.

His standard rant delivered, he got up, nodded to the two nurses over in another booth, and left his table cluttered with his lunch items.

"*Doctors never cleaned up after themselves either,*" he said to himself, as if that kind of behavior was common and the accepted norm.

He left the small cafeteria, went down the main dome tunnel past administration and other offices, and then turned into the patient areas. Here, he glanced into some of the recovery rooms and saw other doctors and staff handling whatever it was they had to. Being a doctor, he knew, was a long,

long road to a life of fulfillment … but one that was clouded with items that the rest of the Issians never had to deal with. Sickness, disease, mental issues, body issues—the list was longer than he even knew. But that was the path he'd chosen those decades ago.

He nodded to an intern he'd watched drain an abscess on a patient just a few days ago and made a note to send through to the attending that the girl had done fine. Perhaps—maybe barely—but perhaps a bit too much bedside manner, which he knew for a female doctor to male patient relationship was often misunderstood by the patient. *"But that story was for another day,"* he said to himself as he turned to leave the in-patient dome and went down the long single corridor to the SecureWard, where he worked most of each day.

He reached the end of the long corridor, lit well from the recessed lighting above tucked away in the ceiling, its matte green deck, floors, and walls all spotless and clean. Moving up to the login panel, he stared straight ahead at the bull's-eye target while the SecureWard AI scanned his retina. A green light now replaced that bull's-eye, and the AI said, "Welcome, Dr. Jack Twelves, please report to the Maternity Ward room number three-one-one-two," and the door ahead of him slid open to admit him.

He nodded, made his way into the secured area,

turned left immediately, and went down another long corridor to move over to the Maternity dome. He smiled as he entered the room. Today was going to be an easy procedure—seeing as all he had to do was to instruct and watch, and he went over to the cleaning station side room.

Scrubbing up and donning a new gown, gloves, and mask, he returned to the room to take stock.

On the table, of course, lay the pregnant patient, but he purposely did not check her chart. *There was no need to know the personal details of either this young woman or her ID. He'd learned long ago, that this was best for him, to be an unknowing participant only.*

Beside her, the anesthesiologist stood, monitoring the patient on his equipment. He gave the doctor a thumbs-up gesture, and that was a good thing.

On either side of the table were the OR nurses again that he didn't know, but then they tended to move about so much up here on the MedWards and down on Eons too, it was a usual thing to be working with strangers.

Above the table on a large monitor, the ultrasound screen showed the patients

At the foot of the table stood the twins.

These two he did know—Inner Circle members Zara and Ella something. He knew that he knew their surname, but he had tried hard to forget it. No need to be that close, and he walked over to the table to stand on the left-hand side of the deeply breathing woman.

"And time line—we're exact on that, agreed?"

The same nurse nodded, looked at the chart to her left, and said, "Guaranteed, Doctor, that she is less than week five."

Good, Jack thought, perfect timing once again.

"What did we use this time?" he asked no one in particular, but the nurse across from him said, "Small growth on her cervix."

When faced with the choice of a simple medical procedure to remove same—as opposed to the fact that such a growth could affect the birth process negatively and in some rare cases, cause a stillborn —the mothers always opted for the simple in-patient clinic procedure. The patient had walked in here today expecting a single child, but Jack knew she'd walk out expecting twins—Issian Inner Circle twins.

He nodded and then said, "Let's get this done, shall we?" He took the remote ultrasound tool handle and slowly drilled down on the embryo as it sat within the patient.

At the foot of the table, Zara and Ella were fixated on that image up on the screen, as Jack moved the apparatus around a bit looking to show the embryo at the best angle, and yes, there it was— the best view.

"We're looking at about a ... say, a less than one-thousand-cell structure," Jack said as he gently moved the reader around the woman's lower abdomen.

"And from the declension of same, I know that the cells are all totipotent, which is what we want. Zara and Ella, you're good to go," he said, as he now locked the ultrasound reader at that viewpoint.

Zara reached for her twin's hand, and together they stared up at the monitor with a focus that was intense.

Nothing happened at first on the screen. Not a hint of movement or for that matter anything at all.

Then, without warning, it was like a line or an edge appeared at the massed cells in the center of that embryo, moving to each side at the same time. As the whole room watched, the one embryo now was split into two, each about the same size, but he knew small variations would not matter.

He looked over at the twins beside him and said, "Time to choose," and then he looked back up at the screen.

The twins were busy continuing to stare at the monitor, but he really had no idea how they could use their minds to sort and to choose from within such a tiny few-celled-sized embryo what to sort, what to move, what to keep, and what to dismiss, yet it always happened right in front of him.

On the screen, smaller than cell-sized structures or pieces or items—whatever one called them, Jack thought–moved from the topside embryo down to the lower one. Karotypes moved to the lower embryo as did chromosomes, genes, and all the parts that makeup an Issian baby. The top cells looked no different, yet they'd been stripped of what would make them another Issian baby.

He looked over at Zara and waited until he got the nod that the twins were done, and then he turned back to the apparatus on the mother's belly. Choosing a new toggle on the remote, he quickly coated both embryos with artificial zona pellucida, and he finished off the making of the twins inside this patient. He slowly disengaged the apparatus and the ultrasound remote too.

Moments later he looked back and noted the twins had left. One of the nurses had stayed around to work with the awakening patient as the anesthesiologist said, "Coming out of it in about five minutes."

Jack stood back as he took off his gloves, snapping them into the organic wastebasket beside him.

"Okay, then when she's awake, wheel her down to recovery—I'll join her there—tell her in about twenty minutes—and explain how she's now carrying twins. Surprise!" he said with a bit of levity in his voice, and he tossed the mask too into the bin and walked out of the Maternity OR.

An hour later, he sat in his small office back in the administration area of the MedWard main dome as he finished his report on the procedure. *Another set of twins. One with all the right items plus all of her sister's too—and one that would be stillborn.*

He electronically signed his report, sent it off encrypted as usual to the Master Adept and her Inner Circle, and half-smiled ... another day that had gone well...

#####

Again, the Master Adept sipped her water and wondered how soon the plans that had been in the making for more than ten years would come together. She bubbled a bit of that mouthful of water under her tongue, enjoying the odd sensation, and then swallowed it completely.

At more than one hundred years old, no one, she thought, *experiences much that's new to them anymore, yet somehow the advances that medical science made had surprised her.*

The fact that she could now control—at least via her plans, which yes, still needed to work out—getting the best and brightest on the Inner Council, which was important. Issians, some only mind you, had always had the potential ability to read the future, use telekinesis, or mind read others close to them physically had always existed. But the new medical advancements allowing them to now split an embryo into twins and then harvest from one twin all those special genes and Karotypes and move them into the only twin that would live was a process she had been quick to use.

We must always try to grow, or we die.

Like Eons itself—almost, she added, knowing that one day the planet's massive blue sun would level out and the climate would return to being normal—or at least better for agriculture, she hoped.

She walked over to the window to look out at the deserted farm that lay to the west. As always, she stared at the barn leaning sickly and the farmhouse without a roof. She stared at the scene that never changed. Barns, farmhouses, corrals, and paddock fences for hundreds, if not thousands, of miles would look the same—long forsaken and left in a state of deterioration.

She looked up at the sky. It was the seventh month, and at this time of the year, that blue sunlight often lit up—yes, there it was. She looked up at the ring that circled Eons. It was thin and yet still a bit shiny in the bright daylight. As Eons in a few of its summer months moved along its orbit, the sun often lit up the single ring that circled the planet. It was better seen on nights when the moon was full, but even so, it was still so natural. Yet, the sunlight that shone down and lit up the ring was the same sunlight that had so severely affected the Eons climate.

Our planet is sick, but we are prospering

It had taken some years of trial—testing on young pregnant women—and many embryos were lost. In the days past, the embryos had been split manually by medical staff, separating the single embryo into two of same, after removing it from the mother in a long and tedious operation. Once out, it used to be that a single Master from the Inner Circle tried to move the items from one embryo to the other. Then the embryo was re-implanted into the mother, and they waited to see what would happen. And as she well knew, the procedures failed for the most part, or the twin that had been stripped of all things that made an Issian a mental power died. Or worse, was born and could be seen to be less than normal.

Moving the work of that separation to twins had been an idea the previous Master Adept had come up with, and she thanked her predecessor for that initiative. It had worked out that twins, both with the needed Master abilities, could do what a single Master could not. Add in the new advances that now allowed this all to be done still in utero, and the chances for success increased exponentially.

They now had more than a dozen of the new ultra-twins living and growing up as Issians.

They had no idea what they were. They had no idea what they were going to be able to accomplish once puberty, and the realizations of who they could be, set in. In just another ten years, she thought, the first of them would be asked to join the Inner Circle, and that would become a self-fulfilling process for the next thousand years.

"Least that is how I see it," she said to herself, as she sat on the small couch near the far wall, faced the doorway, and waited.

A minute later, the door opened and in came an aide, who bowed once to her and stood in front of her.

"Master, you wanted to know more about three things, and I have the information for you," she said and closed her mouth. There was no more need to talk.

The Master nodded, then peered into her aide's mind, and saw what she wanted to know.

Captain Tanner Scott was ensconced into the academy facilities and had already made some real efforts in getting things squared away. That was a sidebar that she was happy to note. She knew he'd been called to Eons, but it was not for any academy work at all. The admiral seemed happy too, which was another extra that she almost grinned at.

Our deal with the Barony to accept their whole naval academy and stitch it into our own—including the enormous payments that went along with that move was a bonus too.

Scott wouldn't know why he was here for quite a while, and yet, it was so nice to see he actually was helping out.

Point two was the recent MedWard twinning, and she had received the full report on her console about that yesterday, but it was also nice to get a direct set of thoughts from the doctor too. Zara and Ella had done well; embryos were both viable, and it would be weeks until testing could tell if the one twin was going to be superior.

Like the rest, she thought and smiled.

And lastly, the third thing she had asked for information about was Kendal Steyn and her group of protesters. *She continued, it appeared, to attract new converts—if you could call a handful of them important to even measure. She too, but thirty years back, had been one of the earliest twinning tests, back when things were done manually. Her twin, however, had not succumbed and been stillborn—hence, her being held up at the Secure MedWards for all these years. Taking the chance to bring Kendal into the Inner Circle had been a major discussion, and finally it was voted down. They could not risk having an Inner Circle member have a twin— even a twin like Mariam who drooled and needed to be*

*fed with a tube—alive. No one knew what that might
cause, so the chance was not taken.*

*Hence, Kendal's pre-occupation with the Twins
Cooperative and her attempts at publicizing something.
She had no inside knowledge of what was being done—
but she still had a few followers.*

The Master Adept shook her head. She now had
the names and information about the newest
members, and she knew that it would be apropos
for them to be contacted in the near future with a
small warning about the Twins Cooperative.
Something negative but not forceful, perhaps just
something about their plans might work.

As she noodled around the thinking on that, she
dismissed her aide who bowed one more time and
left the living area of the tower. A plan was needed
to start to derail the Twins Cooperatives small
success in growth.

#####

As she lay in her bed, tossing first one way and
then the other, Kendal knew it was coming once
again.

The restlessness that she felt was the one thing
that always heralded an upcoming session with
Miriam, and she propped up an extra pillow behind
her head. From here, she couldn't see outside to the
garden at the back of the house—that untended and

sadly neglected garden. From here, she could see
the small alley that ran beside her little bungalow
and the total lack of traffic at this late night hour.
Sometimes, there were walkers who strode by, in an
attempt to walk to healthiness, while other times
those small electric trikes cruised by, carrying folks
home from a night out over in the main dome of
Aporia. Above her, the planet itself was almost
hidden, but she could still see a section of the
planet's ring, shining in the moonlight like a tiara
over Eons.

*Living here in the far west dome was a pleasure if you
wanted privacy, something Kendal wished she could have
right now,* as her left leg cramped up and she gasped
as the muscles contracted suddenly.

Miriam was there, in her mind, screaming at her. The
twin that somehow had not been stillborn, but those
thirty-some odd years ago been birthed alive,
screamed at Kendal, and the words were full of
hate.

She writhed on her bed in the MedWard secure
wing; her left foot and its long toenails scrabbled at
the sheet and even tore it somewhat. Her arms were
pinned—restrained they called it—so that she
couldn't move her torso very much, but it was still
arched up and lifted right off the bed. Her neck was
twisted up to support her head, and from her
mouth, the almost inhuman cries were coming out

as loud as she could yell.

One fingernail on her right hand had not been very closely trimmed, and she sunk that nail into the palm of her hand and drew blood. The nail dug deeper and deeper, and blood now dripped onto the floor, notifying the AI that there was an issue in the room with the patient. She even had a couple of inches of free movement as she whipped that arm back and forth all the time.

She screamed even louder, her eyes shut as tightly as possible.

"I want them dead! I want them to die! I want them to be tied to this bed for thirty years … I want them dead!" she screamed over and over.

Kendal reached over for the other pillow and jammed it over her head, but it was impossible to drown out her twin's screams. Whatever Miriam yelled, she heard full volume in her own head. Whatever Miriam felt body-wise, she too felt and knew that when they added extra sedation to Miriam's IV, the cramps would go away and her own body would relax in sync with Miriam's body.

She could not speak back to Miriam—she could only receive these unholy rants from her twin, and she only wished that she could do that.

Kendal twisted as the cramp in her side deepened and her breathing grew shallower until that cramp went away.

In the MedWard secure administration center, a nurse looked at the chart of the patient she'd just been notified about and noted the huge red border around the NO CONTACT orders. But there was blood on the floor, and that meant that the patient would need, even at a minimum, some kind of cleaning and bandaging. So she ignored the standing orders and clicked through to the AI that she wanted access to the patient's room. Walking down the corridor all the way to the end, she stopped only to grab a cart with first aid equipment. At the door to the patient's room, she palmed the security plate to allow herself access and went in to see the patient.

Inside she was shocked even more at the appearance of the patient; the vids back in administration hadn't captured just how bad off this woman looked, as she moved over to the right-hand side of the bed and down at the floor.

The patient's mouth was wide open, but in a silent scream, the nurse thought, as she stooped to wipe up the few drops of blood. As she rose, the patient's right hand grabbed at her neck, seizing it in a grasp that was like a vise.

The nurse almost choked as the fingers tightened severely around her windpipe, and it was only with both hands that she was able to unlock those fingers from her throat.

She stepped back and shook her head; *this was truly a patient from hell.* As she made a large change in the IV sedative dosages, the patient quickly lay back down at rest instead of fighting it all.

Looking at the palm of the patient's right hand was easy. After she cinched up the restraints as tight as they could be, she quickly daubed the deep cut with water to wash it and then an antiseptic spray, and finally she pressed a self-adhesive bandage over the whole palm.

She took note of the time for her report and then left the patient's room, towing the cart behind her.

Kendal, of course, had seen all of this, and as Miriam began to quiet, the link with her twin lessened.

She sent her love and told her for the millionth time that she'd see her twin freed somehow … someday …

CHAPTER FOUR

Twisting the flyer into a shallow dive, Tanner dropped her down, as if he was a pilot with thousands of hours of stick-time, in the landing port at Tower Number Two. "Not that there even was a stick," he said to himself, "but still, the flyer was fun." Too bad the job ahead looked so daunting.

He nodded once more to the Provost guard at the edge of the landing tarmac and walked toward the massive wide-open doors of the Tower. After reading the reports that had flooded his console over at his office at the Eons landing port, he knew this one was supposedly the worst off when it came to occupancy permits. Everything was behind, everything had been short-shipped, and from what he'd been able to determine off the monitor reports, everyone was blaming everyone else.

He nodded to a couple of cadets, who were slugging cartons up the stairs to the front deck off the doors and loading dollies at the same time. Cases already stacked said that they held classroom desks, ready to be assembled, made he noted over on Amasis, the big Barony manufacturing world. *Good to know,* he thought, and he walked by the long lineup of dollies.

At least, goods were being delivered—though why it'd be such a big thing in his earlier read reports that they weren't. That needed a look-see too, he thought, and he wandered into the enormous lobby rotunda.

Here, as this was such a major student area, there would be—well, there was in fact, a large greeting reception area with a round circular table that must have been fifty feet across, supported by what would eventually be receptionists helping cadets find their way. Or visitors. Or tourists maybe, and at that he smiled, but he pushed away any thoughts of wide-eyed tourists at a naval academy.

He went over to a sergeant in the Provost guards and said, "Excuse me, Sergeant?"

"Don't wanna hear it, I've no bloody idea, Cadet, where anything goes!" he barked before he turned around, but once he saw a full captain behind him, he snapped to attention.

"Sir, apologies—didn't know it was you, Sir. Just that the cadets all seem to not know—"

"Yes, Sergeant, I got it. Not a problem. I just wanted to know where the admin for this tower would be located?" Tanner asked nicely. The guard was obviously fed up with questions about things he had no idea about, hence the quick reply, but that didn't matter to him.

The guard nodded and then pointed to the far glass wall that peeked from behind the rows of boxes lined up against it.

"Behind that glass doorway, Sir—down to the second door to starboard, Sir," he replied.

Tanner nodded and smiled. "Remember, Sergeant, most of these cadets are new to life—let alone new to Tower Number Two ... do cut them a bit of slack—as a personal favor to me, Sergeant?" he asked nicely.

And he received a nod, a salute, and a snappy "Yes, Captain" in return.

He walked by the bank of elevators, noting that here due to the huge influx of student cadets that would occur daily, someone had put in twelve elevators, which was a good thing. He also noted there wasn't single piece of that yellow tape that showed an elevator was closed, and that too was a good thing—and that did get a smile from him, the elevator whisperer indeed!

He looked again at the cases that were stacked up. Several of them were labeled as classroom desks, again from Amasis, and after a quick count, he realized there were at least a thousand of same here in the lobby. That did seem odd, but then he really had no idea as to the total number needed above, so he filed that away for later double-checking.

Finding the edge of the glass wall was easy, as it jutted out from tall boxes stacked horizontally that claimed to be white boards. He went in through the opening in the glass wall. Doors to come later, he theorized and went down the hallway to the second door to the right and through the opening there too.

What was ahead of him was perhaps typical of what one might find on a job site, but Tanner still stopped cold.

A series of doors, many doors, were stacked up to form makeshift desks on which lay reams and reams of blueprints and wide paper architectural design layouts. Some were being held down by cans of paint so that they didn't roll up while others had hard hats doing the holding. Few of the tables didn't have someone staring down at them, but the big central table made from double doors had a group of five construction workers, all staring and talking. No one paid any attention to him at all, as he walked in to stand opposite the big central table.

"Can't be. Can't be out by two feet on the bias, Bill. Best thing is to re-check the Add-On checklist and see—as I remember about four months ago, we got an Add-On to change those dimensions all across floor thirteen," one said as he pointed at something on the blueprints.

"Oh, it's two feet all right—two goddamn bloody feet that means that the whole lecture theater will be minus one hundred and twenty feet lengthwise, so that means, what, ten less students? Theaters to all be the same, student total—and this one is out," another said.

"Which means we steal two feet from the other side, then two from the next three theaters all the way to the east side services corridor, and that'll do that," Bill, the one wearing the pressed shirt, said as an answer.

They all stopped talking and started pointing. They seemed to lean back a bit to digest this idea, and in doing so, a couple of them looked up at Tanner.

"Uh—Sir? Can we help you?" one of them said.

Tanner just stared at them all and then focused on the head man who'd spoken.

"Is this solution pretty normal?" he asked, which got a frown on just about every face.

One of the men laid a hand out to stop anyone else from talking.

"And you, Sir are ...?" he asked, his tone not quite insulting but definitely superior. He was about fifty years old with a clean-shaven face and balding head with little gray wisps of hair and a nice clean pressed shirt. No nametag or rank showed on the man—he was a civilian for sure, and Tanner suspected he was the head of the construction crew here at Tower Number Two.

He smiled but made sure to wipe it off his face almost immediately.

"I am Captain Tanner Scott—2IC here on Eons for the new academy build. So you report to me, I'd think. And again, my question is—does this kind of workaround for construction problems happen often—and is the answer I just heard the one you're going to go with?" he said, his voice flat and hard.

The man didn't flinch. Didn't react at all. He stood there for about a half a minute, processing what he'd just heard, Tanner imagined, and then spoke up.

"Doubt you're my boss, Captain. But yes, this kind of thing does happen—building four brand new towers each with over seven hundred thousand square feet of space to design, build, then equip is a lengthy job. Add to that, that the designs you see here," he said as he tapped the wad of blueprints on the makeshift table in front of them, "get changed almost weekly—Add-Ons, we call them. Move that wall on foot east to now meet with bulkhead J-34GT6 kind of thingy. And then they get changed again and again. It's like trying to hit a moving target ... all invisible when the building is up and occupied, Captain. So yes, what we are now considering is to not affect the size of a lecture theater—to keep its student population size what was asked for—demanded in fact—by making changes in a side corridor. Do you follow me, Captain?" he said, and he crossed his arms on his chest.

Defensive body language, Tanner thought, but still he had to agree when he heard the truth.

"My apologies if I sounded adversarial, but I am your boss. And yes, I know what you just said was both pragmatic and truthful at the same time. Carry on—and I'd sign off on the change you just made too, if you'd care to know," he added.

The man looked happy and held out his hand as a token of respect. "Captain Scott—I'm Superintendent Bill Chapman—glad to meet you. And thanks!" he added as they shook hands.

Tanner nodded to them all and then went out of the administration area and to the elevators.

He hitched a ride up to floor thirteen and noted as he got off that he could hear power tools being used in many locations on this floor. Moving to his far left, he went down a corridor that ran parallel to the tower wall and slowly moved its full length. From what he could see, the eight-foot-wide corridor on the east side of the tower was fine. If this was the corridor that would end up being only six feet wide—to accommodate the full lecture theaters—then that change was fine. Small rooms were off the corridor, most likely he thought for janitorial, IT, and quartermaster stores, and that didn't need a full eight feet of clearance in the corridor.

Least, I hope not, he reasoned, as he turned back to the elevator area and then picked a lecture theater to enter.

Moving through the doorway that actually had doors, which was a surprise, he entered and then stopped at the top of the aisle ahead that moved down almost thirty feet via landings. Each landing level had an arc of desks, already assembled and placed in a long row pointing down to the stage area below. There were ten of those rows and desks, and he didn't bother to count, but he saw that a two-foot section, cut off one whole side wall, would decrease the number of students by ten students.

"Good workaround," he said to himself, and in his book, that Chapman fellow went up a notch…

"*Is this—*" the woman in labor groaned, "what it's always like or just 'cause I'm having twins?"

She moved her one foot in the stirrups farther in same, and the nurse beside her reached up to massage the foot a bit as it was obvious that it was cramping up.

She twisted her pelvis, but she couldn't really get away from the pain of childbirth—agonizing contractions that were only barely lessened with the spinal epidural. She knew, or thought she knew, that her whole lower half was cramped up with the expansion seizures that went along with the widening of the birth canal.

"Same for all pregnant women," the nurse, who was seated between her legs monitoring the births, said. "Twins come out one at a time. Active one first always ... and that paves the way for girl number two," she added and noted that the cervix had only three inches of dilation but that effacement was about one hundred percent.

Oblivious to the technical end of what childbirth was all about, the mother groaned and said, "More drugs ... this is so, so, so bad."

All in the labor and delivery room nodded, but she didn't get any more drugs. The anesthesiologist said, "Yes, ma'am" and then did nothing but move around behind the sheet that hid the mother's body from the equipment up at the head of the delivery table.

She yelped right out loud, and the groans that

came next paralleled the dilation of her cervix even more, and the nurse between her legs said over her shoulder, "Call Dr. Twelves."

Ten minutes later, a gowned and masked man came in and smiled at the woman in labor though she couldn't see it because of that mask.

"Helen, you're doing fine—been monitoring you from the labor and delivery room computer, and all is well. You'll be outta here with a set of twins in no time," he said as he lied to her.

Mask helps a bit, he thought. Lying is always difficult during the birth but was a part of the overall twins program.

He replaced the nurse between the woman's legs and gently palpated the woman's pelvis and pressed down slightly on the womb as well.

"Hot compress for the perineum, please," he said as one was handed to him by one of the nurses. The perineum was the major source of the stretching to accompany the birth as the woman's first twin began to crown.

"A nice gentle push, please, Helen," the doctor said as he slowly grasped the first twin's head and manipulated the baby's body to slightly turn to one side.

"And another too," he said as the woman groaned and her feet trembled in the stirrups above the bed, but push she did.

And the twin was born. The healthy and live twin.

He twisted slightly on his stool and carefully handed the girl to one of the nurses who bustled it over to a warming station for cleanup and inspection.

One down — the easy one, Dr. Twelves thought and sighed mentally.

"Okay, Helen, how about number two, now." He knew this one would be different.

As the pregnant woman's body moved to expel the next child, he helped as much as he could. He gave his high sign to the anesthesiologist who added a healthy increase to the woman's IV line to quiet her a bit more, and he waited.

He knew, as did all involved in the labor and delivery room, *that about fifteen to twenty minutes would be the norm for the second birth, so he was happy to have the time to chat a bit with the woman.*

As the first twin was now ready to be united with the woman, he held off on that for a bit and looked down to see the second twin's head, crowning in the birth canal opening.

He knew his touch could not be seen nor felt as he slid the forceps in and simply grabbed the head of the second baby and then applied a steady pulling to extract it.

He knew when to say "What?" out loud, and he

knew when to add "Nurse, get me a cart," and he knew when to hold down the woman's pelvis as she became aware that something was wrong.

Twisting the stillborn child first left and then right got the body out of the woman, and he quickly dropped the forceps, handled the baby with respect, got up, and ran over to the warming station.

He did what all medical doctors would do then—knowing that the labor and delivery security cameras caught all of this—and he knew that what would happen was what was planned to happen.

The second twin was a stillborn child.

It was not alive.

He had learned this just a few weeks back when the woman had had her final tests before birth.

According to plan, the lesser of the two twins was not allowed to be born alive.

He worked quickly using all of the normal medical tricks to try to revive the child—but it had been dead for weeks.

Killed by the other twin, he knew—but only he knew that. The mother and the labor and delivery staff would never know that.

He heard the sobs of the woman and nodded to one of the nurses to take over the living twin and place it on the mother's breasts. The woman grabbed her child and cried as he explained at her side that sometimes—not often at all, but sometimes

—these things happened. The stillborn child had died just before childbirth as the nuchal cord cut off the blood flow to the child.

She sobbed. He made excuses. The nurses went on with their cleanups, and the anesthesiologist slowly disengaged his equipment and let the doctor know he was done.

She cried yet the tears were subsiding—she had a brand new daughter in her arms.

Time would help heal this, Twelves knew.

Time would allow her to slowly forget what she had lost and enjoy what she had just been given.

Time would also allow the surviving twin to prosper, to grow, and to one day become a member of the Inner Circle.

He smiled as he patted the woman's shoulder as they wheeled her out of the labor and delivery room.

An EYES ONLY to the Master Adept would be his last chore of the day, reporting on the success of the birth of a new candidate for her Inner Circle— years away, but still a task that was important

As Tanner strode down the hallway and made the left into the final corridor that led to his office, he glanced in at the admiral's area as he went by. Inside the wide-open door, Lieutenant Kelsey

CoSharan was standing up at his filing cabinet, his tail stuck out straight. Trouble city, Tanner knew, accompanied that placement of the Faraway alien's tail. *"Hope it's not me,"* he said to himself, as he grinned and walked down to the last door on the right.

No need to lock anything, he realized as the door slid open and he went in to get to work early this morning. "Backpack here," he said to himself as he took out the container of yogurt and the small pack of fruit to sprinkle on same he'd picked up over at the Officers' Mess this morning. *No idea what kind of fruit this is,* he thought as he looked down at the circles of green tart flesh with the halo of dark seeds in a circle near the center. He undid the yogurt container, plopped in those green fruit circles, and began to eat as he held a thumb over the monitor plate for his ID recognition.

"Beep," echoed from the computer, and he found he had more than forty-seven messages—most with the MOST IMPORTANT icons flashing in their margins.

He sighed, had another big spoonful of yogurt, and enjoyed the tart fruit add-ins.

"Number one," he said to himself and noted it was from some professor in the astrophysics area, who was requesting an immediate stoppage of work in his office so that he could get a wall moved so that he could get a larger view-screen on the wall. *"Not a chance,"* he said to himself and sent back his standard boilerplate message: We've got your message and are considering same. By the time the professor could mount any kind of a problem, the walls would be in and the message moot.

He nodded, archived the message in his DONE folder, and went to number two.

Yogurt's good today, he thought, and he went through his messages one by one by one.

Most were the same; issues with personal requests for changes to various offices, rooms, lecture theaters, and even a couple for more bathroom hand dryers. He shook his head at that *and wondered if the professor who'd asked twice for that was from Elbo—complete with six arms.* That got a smile, and he again sent his standard answer, and the message went into the DONE folder.

One message, about midway through the list, was from the Master Adept—or an aide perhaps— requesting a time to meet with him in the near future. *No real rush,* it read, but he answered personally and offered up a couple of times early next week to meet. And the reply went out.

Further issues included a request for a color change in white boards—to teal blue, which he thought was dumb, but then he supposed this professor had a reason why that was a necessary change, but it escaped him. *Denied.*

One asked for a double-parking spot for his flyer —as he liked to not allow other flyers close to his own craft as it was a vintage R-989 Turbo model— whatever the hell that was. *Denied.*

One asked for a change in the first semester start date—obviously, the towers were not going to be completed, so let's move back the date was the rationale. *Denied,* but he might have enjoyed okaying that one.

One asked for more signs to be posted on a floor when the bots were doing cleanup so that she couldn't fall down again—he wondered at that but made a note to check to see just how that was handled. *Handled.*

One asked for upgraded access to the network via his console to be installed in his office, claiming that without same, he couldn't use the office AI to tap into his favorite vid programs. At least he was honest about goofing off and wanting to lie on his couch to watch programs that had nothing to do with the academy. *Denied.*

Tanner slowly worked through the lengthy list, and he finished the yogurt at about the same time, tossing the empty container and spoon into his trashcan. Just finding a trashcan yesterday had been a challenge, as he had to walk and peer into other offices for doubles of same. Not finding any, he then tried up on the second floor of the administration building in some of the unassigned offices, and he'd found a stash of more than a dozen in one corner. So he liberated one, and now it sat under his desk with the used yogurt container in it.

He stood, went over to the window, and looked out onto the vast landing field that stretched out before him.

One new ship had arrived overnight—a cruiser from the Duchy d'Avigdor—the *GoldEye*—and she was busy getting off-loaded with cargo. He noted that the bot-trucks were stacked with cases that he knew looked familiar and wondered what the Duchy d'Avigdor had just provided for the academy towers. Something needed, he hoped, and his attention was suddenly moved over across the landing port to another pad. As usual, on all RIM Confederacy planet landing fields, sub-sonic klaxons were sounded all over a landing pad when a ship was coming down to roost. Lights from each corner of the pad lit up, and you just had to pay attention.

From above, on a downward flight path, a Barony ship—the *BN Whitney*, a cruiser he'd never been on before—was dropping onto the pad. Down, down it came, its own momentum carefully managed by whomever was at the helm, and the crewman was doing an artful job, Tanner noted, as the helm spun the ship about thirty degrees to point its large cargo holds more directly toward the terminal. Well done, he thought, as the *Whitney* slowly dropped onto her large landing fins and the ship settled in place.

All of us, RIM-wide, he thought, *are involved in the building of the new academy—at least from what I can see. Barony too*, he noted, as he tried to shy away from even thinking about why he'd been shanghaied into his current posting.

Fool with a Royal and you paid a price. But he said cautiously to himself, "I'd not fooled at all."

"In fact," he said as he realized that it was true, "I had fallen for Helena."

But not Royal life.

Impasse. Checkmate. Mexican standoff, whatever it was called, he had a problem.

And the problem was his and his alone.

So, I wonder what I can do to—

"Captain?" the admiral said as he strode into Tanner's office, "I need to give you these idiot—uh, not so good—items for your touch with same. I'm tired of trying to walk the tightrope between political correctness and showing idiots the door. Handle them as you see fit ..."

He dropped a large stack of paper requests for changes onto Tanner's desk, turned curtly, and left as quickly as he'd appeared.

Tanner nodded, said to the back of his boss, "Aye, Sir," and then shook his head at the height of the stack.

All professors were supposed to use the online request queue—but some, as he could see, would rather use old-fashioned memos.

All would be handled and all would not be honored in any way, he thought. As usual. At least so far.

He smiled, sat at his desk, and wondered when he'd get to leave today.

Late probably, as usual.

Ahh, the life of a bureaucrat means keeping one eye on the clock …

She turned to face Gillian directly and even half-smiled as she clouded her thoughts enough so that her Adept officer couldn't really see what she was thinking. The fact that Gillian knew she was hiding something was obvious to them both and yet it went unspoken.

She cleared her throat for a second and then began.

"Gillian, I've been thinking about the secondment of Captain Scott over to Eons. And I'm wondering if you can provide me with more information on that—as it was your own idea to do this?" she said.

And it was true. While Helena had wished him some kind of punishment, Gillian had presented the idea that a tour of duty over on Eons, looking after all of those vexatious, small, and seemingly never-ending set of tasks, would do nicely.

She wondered for a moment if that were true, but she held her gaze solidly on Gillian as they sat in her quarters.

Today was an apricot day: leggings and soft, soft Garnuthian leather boots in a dull apricot color, topped with an apricot short jacket and blouse with a shine that almost hurt one's eyes. Her hair, long and blonde, had been done by her hairdresser just an hour ago, and the hints of apricot-colored streaks in some of her locks set off her whole look.

Gillian nodded and held out both hands, palms up. "Helena—you did think at the time that this was a great idea for what we called punishment, Ma'am. And to be honest, Ma'am, I was only the messenger on this plan—it came from my Master Adept. And as I mentioned at the time, this was run by the Baroness too, who left the decision up to you," she added, pulled her hands back in, and leaned back in her chair.

Helena stared at her for a moment and then asked with a tone that was polite yet undeniably firm, "And is the captain enjoying his banishment to

Eons so far?" She wanted to know and that could not be hidden from Gillian anymore, who nodded.

"Ma'am, it appears that your captain is good at the tasks needed to be helpful in the academy move to the new towers," she said.

"And further, he also appears to be doing little else, I'm told. He goes in early and comes back to his billet later than most, and so far, as I said, he's been good at handling the various factors that crop up daily. Or so I'm told.

"But I can tell you the whole construction and equipping of the towers is way behind, schedule-wise. Issues with suppliers and equipment and inspectors happen every day. Most wonder if they'll even hit the deadlines to begin the first semester in about two months' time, Ma'am."

Helena twirled a strand of her apricot-dyed hair and frowned at the same time. "So, good at destroying Pirates and killing rioters—who knew he'd also be good at something so mundane as well," she said, and even she could hear the frustration in her voice.

Gillian sat quietly and waited. She knew more was to come.

Helena looked at the view-screen, which now had a slide show of the beautiful Randi waterfalls—white flowing water falling thousands of feet through holes in a cliff or rushing down a set of step-like rock terraces. The falls on Randi were beautiful, and she made a point to try to get to Randi to see them in person sometime in the near future. After a few minutes of appreciating the waterfall, she looked over at Gillian.

"I want to go to Eons to visit this new academy. I will ask Rear Admiral Higgins if he can assign Captain Scott to be my guide for the tour so that I can learn more about how he's handling this tour of duty. We're off Roor, are we not?" she asked.

"Ma'am, could I perhaps ask for a delay for this trip—at least for two months to the start of their first semester? Going now would only show you all of the problems and issues—ones that your captain handles daily," Gillian asked nicely.

Helena shook her head. "We go now, Gillian—end of story."

"Yes, Ma'am. About thirty days from Eons—which would get us there during the final month of the tower construction and all," Gillian said smartly.

Helena nodded. "Then I'll tell the bridge to get us to Eons, and thank you, Gillian, for your counsel today," she said.

Hadn't been much counsel, Helena thought, but she'd needed to just bounce her idea off someone.

Gillian nodded and retired to pass along the new information about the upcoming visit of the Lady

St. August to Eons. She wondered how the Master Adept was going to handle that, but she shook her head.

Way above my pay grade, she thought.

CHAPTER FIVE

Within the small commercial building with Twins Cooperative painted on the glass storefront windows, a set of twins waited in the reception area. They had been sitting now for over an hour, and while their appointment time was well past, they continued to wait.

One of them, the one with the magenta jacket, sat tapping a foot, obviously not happy with the wait but unwilling to ask yet again what the holdup was. Her twin, dressed in robin's egg blue, sat quietly, eyes closed, staring at the inside of her eyelids in a calm manner. Twins, yes, but different twins as they were fraternal twins not identical twins.

An assistant, who worked in a back office area, came out to see them yet again and offered a refill on their tea or perhaps a bottle of water, and both were again politely refused by the twins.

From another inner office, a door opened up loudly and a shrill yelling voice rang out.

"I'm telling you—it was her! I know my twin and it was her, and yet she's been gone for years. Yet there she was on the street, walking and window shopping—but by the time I could get the bus to stop and get off and run back to that spot, she disappeared," the young woman cried out.

She stomped out from the back area, and all could see that she was upset as she loudly proclaimed that she had just seen her twin.

Kendal trailed after her, nodding and putting a hand on the upset woman's shoulder, trying to calm her, but she was having none of it.

"You said that couldn't happen—you said that they had taken away my twin—yet there she was, shopping on the street. I know my twin—even though she died—and yet there she was. And you said they'd killed her, and yet there she was—I saw her just yesterday ..." the woman sobbed, falling into Kendal's arms in grief.

Kendal nodded, stroked the woman's hair, and tried to comfort her as best she could.

"Yes, Joy, yes ... I know ..." she said over and over, leading the woman slowly back toward an inner office to comfort her in private.

The assistant looked at the twins still waiting,

smiled, and went back to her own area behind reception, while the office quieted once more.

Twenty more minutes passed, and then the upset woman, now quite calm, walked by and out the front door, while Kendal approached the two waiting women in reception.

"I am so, so sorry about that. But I do thank you for your patience. Please follow me," she said as she led the way to a side meeting room and sat at the round table within. She had a tablet and entered something as the two fraternal twins doffed their jackets and sat before her.

She looked at them and smiled. "That was very unusual, but a part, I'm afraid, of what we see often here at the Twins Cooperative group," she said calmly, knowing there would be more questions.

One twin nodded but asked, "What was that all about?" Her voice was polite but searching for an answer.

Kendal nodded. "Twins face a lot in our Issian society—you as twins, even though just fraternal twins, would know that already. One thing that is, or rather was, unknown is that sometimes—very seldom, mind you—after medical procedures, the Capgras Syndrome can occur," she said as she shook her head.

"Sorry, but what is that?" the other twin asked.

Kendal nodded and sat back as she turned off her

tablet. "Sometimes, a person who is undergoing a medical procedure that requires anesthesia, you know, putting the patient to sleep, requires that Ketamine be used—it's a drug. The woman you just saw—yes, a twin too—has asthma, and last week she needed to have an outpatient procedure done to clear up her increased bronchial secretions. They used Ketamine, as it is one of the best drugs to use as it suppresses breathing so much less than other anesthesia drugs. However, what sometimes in some limited cases happens is that Ketamine can cause hallucinations—and what is also called the Capgras Syndrome. This occurs when a person— this twin—meets or sees someone and they suffer from a delusional misidentification. For instance, where you suddenly believe that your wife or your child has been replaced with an identical copy or clone. It's not your wife but an exact duplicate. Happens rarely but it does happen. In this woman's case, as she had a twin that died a few years ago, the delusions that she got from the asthma procedure last week meant that she identified a woman on the street—a stranger—as her dead twin sister," Kendal said as she shook her head slightly.

"Happens—and as we are all about twins here at the Cooperative, she came here looking for help. I am sorry to say that when we explained, and we requested verifications by her own doctor about the Capgras Syndrome, she was saddened but did see the truth. I suspect that she'd have been much happier to have her twin back—but that, of course, is impossible."

Kendal looked at the twins in front of her and smiled. "Being a twin often has issues that go beyond the 'do we both wear the robin's egg blue outfits today' type of item, don't they?" and that got a nod from both of them.

"Will she be all right?" one said.

Kendal nodded. "Yes, as soon as she realized that this was a result of medication used in her procedure, she calmed, and she has a new appointment with her doctor, as I said, to verify all of this."

The twin who sat with the magenta jacket over her lap leaned in. "We'd like to know more about the Twins Cooperative and how we might help here too," she said and her sister, sitting beside her, patted her on her thigh.

"Right," Kendal said, as she rebooted her tablet and clicked some buttons. The view-screen on the near wall lit up with the Twins Cooperative logo of two twins entwined in the womb. As she clicked more buttons, a video played, and they all watched it as it explained the Twins Cooperatives goals and ambitions…

#####

On Neria, at their landing port, the ramp down to the tarmac wasn't quick enough to just walk on, as the Caliph trotted at full gait to get off the *Roc,* his personal destroyer. The fact that he'd left the most recent RIM Confederacy Executive Committee meeting where he'd been thwarted at every turn by both the Master Adept and the Baroness was jammed in his gut.

The Baroness had said—inferred perhaps might be a better way to have stated her position—that she would be willing to talk to him about the Ikarian longevity vaccine. She had it. It worked and he also knew that testing on criminals over on Halberd, the RIM prison planet, had been successful too. But she also knew that he had at least the same basic formulations—stolen from the Barony Hospital Ship just a year ago. But so far, his medical labs had not been able to duplicate the same results in their testing.

We have it—and we don't. But she didn't know that. I played that card correctly, he thought. Still, she and the Master had forced him to accept that the Ikarian vaccine would be held off any public release until further testing was done.

He knew what that meant. *Yes, there'd be more testing, but at the same time, when those results were complete and the vaccine passed with flying colors, the first initial doses would go to Barony and Eons.*

The Baroness, as far as he could guess, was in her prime—so adding a few hundred years to that would be deadly. She ran ten planets now—had taken over his vice chairman's position as the number two realm in the Confederacy. What she could accomplish in two hundred more years was unthinkable—he had to get the vaccine usable himself by his own labs.

As he bounced into the seat of his scrambler, he quickly pushed the start button and dropped her into first. The tri-wheeled bike zipped away from the landing ramp on the Roc. He powered her up quickly, and the gate guard, knowing who was coming at him with no intention of stopping, hoisted the bar across the road, and Sharia flew by. Turning at the intersection ahead, he quickly passed all the slower traffic illegally in the left-hand lane and then took a side street at quite a clip in a left-hand turn that almost defied gravity. The scrambler tipped up onto only two of its large, knobby wheels, but it kept its footing as ahead loomed yet another gate, but this one was solid wood and steel.

Lifting one hand off the handlebars, the Caliph thumbed a button on the gas tank that lay in front of him, and the message was sent as to who was approaching, and the gates ahead slid back noiselessly. He flew through the gateway, acknowledging his Ramat guardsmen with a quick salute, and then settled in for the three-mile trip across the small dunes to the Caliphate palace ahead.

Palace, he thought as the scrambler climbed first one dune and then flew down another, *is what it's called, but in fact it's a huge conglomeration of tents and buildings and service areas, all intertwined with sheltered walkways and even tunnels.*

Home is another word for it; he liked that better, and that thought got a real smile from him.

He pushed the scrambler for even more speed, remembering that the tri-wheel suspension needed at least some purchase all the time on at least two of its wheels. He'd dumped scramblers before, but not this time. He made a small directional correction to his left to keep the single front wheel still on the hard-packed sands as he came over the top of an angled dune.

She hit hard, but the correction kept him on course and upright, and he slowed as he came around to the side of the palace to park his bike at arrival on the tarmac of the parking area.

A Ramat guard snapped to attention and half-smiled at his Caliph. "Caliph, I see that she handled well." As the guard who had worked on this area of the Palace for over twenty years, he knew his Caliph.

Sharia nodded and said, "She went well—but could you get someone to just check the back end, left side, cables? When I had to brake to avoid a delivery truck back in town, she pulled left ... so ...?"

The guard nodded and gave a brisk salute too. "I will look after that myownself, Caliph, and test it too. She'll be ready for the next time you want to use her, Caliph." He bowed his head slightly.

Sharia nodded as he strode off the tarmac and entered the tenting to gain access to the Caliphate Palace. Another Ramat guard nodded to him and made some kind of notation on the entrance kiosk console. Sharia strode down the long brown-tented corridor. As usual, the corridor was setup to function only as a way to get from the parking area through to the central lobby area of the big building ahead, so it had no art and no style—not a thing but plain tiled floor and the brown tent walls.

"Should do something about that," he said to himself and then realized he had other things to worry about at present.

In the lobby, his aides and his chief of staff, who knew he was expected, met him, and they took a centralized new corridor out of the lobby toward the inner areas of the palace.

"Caliph, I did get your Ansible EYES ONLY

and have assembled the lab team as per your request—they await you in the green room, Caliph," his chief of staff said.

Green room, indeed. If it was one thing that all his subjects knew, it was that the green room was so alien to Neria, a desert planet, that using it meant something was faulty. Something was wrong. Something was in your future and it spelled trouble.

He nodded. *Green room, indeed.*

Back in his inner palace quarters, he changed and refreshed himself with a brisk shower first. "One thing about being the Caliph means I can ignore all the issues about water," he said to himself as the spray in the large plas-glass-walled shower sprayed down on him. He toweled quickly and then put on a clean and well-pressed brown arjack, fresh leggings, and his traditional polished indigo blue boots. At six feet five inches tall, he was average height for a Nerian. He checked out his image in the mirror and ran a set of fingers through his coal-black hair instead of looking for a comb.

He nodded to himself. A Caliph for sure, and then he strode out of his Royal bathroom to leave his quarters and then down a side corridor that not many even knew existed toward the green room. No art in this one either, he realized, but there were a couple of consoles and monitors as sometimes he had needed to check on something before attending meetings and the like.

At a plain wall in front of him, he swept up the tent wall, and it revealed another corridor, much bigger, and as he stepped into same, the brown tent wall behind him dropped back into place. Now a quick right-hand turn, followed by a walk, and, the tenting stopped as he entered a new palace building and a couple of doorways to a green door, which led to the green room.

He stopped to gather his thoughts, but the overall failure of this team to produce results—desired results—flooded over him.

He nodded to his chief of staff, who'd been waiting for him to get here, and they went in together, crossing the floor to the large table that sat in the middle of the large room.

Already seated were eleven members of the Ikarian vaccine team and their leader, Doctor Bassim Najada, who stood up immediately when Sharia entered the room. The rest of the doctor's team stood as well. They all watched as Sharia and his chief took up their positions at the far end of the rectangular table and waited, still standing quietly.

After a moment of looking down at the tablet his chief had slid in front of him, Sharia looked up at the team leader.

They'll stand, he thought as he said politely but with a hint of threat, "Doctor Najada—I have read your reports—yours and your teams as well. You have failed to find me a stable, working vaccine. Have I stated that correctly, Doctor?"

Sharia knew he was right. He also knew that by phrasing his question this way, the doctor had no way to spin his answer either.

The doctor stared at him for a moment and then nodded. "Caliph—yes, exactly. We, so far, have not found a working formulation that has passed all its tests—"

Before the spin came, the Caliph held up his hand. "Doctor, might I offer that I am therefore not happy. Not happy at all, as you have had more than a year with the best lab and equipment that you said you wanted and needed, and you and your team have failed?" Sharia said, and he then pointed a finger at the rest of the team.

"Perhaps that's it, Doctor. You have a team member, or even members, who have failed us— point them out, Doctor, and they'll be on the next freighter to Neria Prime and a life of being an ore miner for the rest of their lives. Who is it, Doctor, that has failed us?" he asked and then leaned back to watch.

Doctor Najada looked at his team members and then back at his Caliph—and he did that a few times.

He's valuing the way out of this, Sharia thought. *He*

could throw a few team members under the bus—and gain time. Or take the blow personally …

The doctor shook his head. "Caliph—that's not it at all. It's just that we have limited resources when it comes to the original supplied sample. We have to grow it very carefully and in acclimatized solutions only—so that all our testing is on the same exact sample. That takes time, Caliph—but I am happy to report that since my report was sent to you just two days ago, yesterday, we found out that a new track may be the way to get some results that are successful, Caliph," he said, his voice full of hope.

Sharia looked at him, took a full minute, and then nodded. "And that would be …"

"The liver, Caliph. We have been led to believe, by our testing, that the liver may be the single functioning host for the vaccine. As you know, the liver has their special Kupffer cells, which eat up and break down the toxins or aging too perhaps, we now think. In short, these cells disarm the toxins by converting a dangerous chemical to a less harmful one or by packaging them for easier disposal through an Ikarian's bile or urine. We think now that this new approach may reveal how the vaccinated liver doesn't always have to fight its enemies head on. Instead, it often uses a martial arts approach and paralyzes toxins by wrapping them in a water-soluble chemical so they land in your toilet rather than in a vital organ, or so we now believe, Caliph."

He was rubbing his hands together, as if he couldn't wait to get back to the labs and get to work, perhaps, the Caliph thought.

"Fine, Doctor. Take your team and find me results that I can use, but I do warn you that Neria Prime will be larger in population if you don't find success soon, Doctor Najada—very, very soon," he finished off.

No one in the room doubted that he meant that.

No one in the room moved.

He nodded and waved his hand at the team, who almost fell over each other to get out of the green room.

He looked at his chief of staff and said, "Identify, say, three of the team who we can send off to Neria Prime who we have replacements available for quickly. No need to do that just yet, but always good to be prepared."

#####

As the *RN Tripp* touched down at the Dessau Naval Base, Tanner and his boss, the Rear Admiral Higgins, walked out slowly to landing pad number thirteen to greet Admiral McQueen, who was here for an inspection of the new academy. Tanner thought—and he was pretty sure that Higgins joined him in this—that the upcoming inspection would find some holes, some jury-rigging, some Rube Goldbergs, and yes, some not-so-good solutions. But he also knew that with only a month left in the allotted time to finish the academy, they were close to making that deadline.

He nodded to the sergeant who drove by slowly to get the visitors' luggage, and as the low truck went by, Higgins said, "Maybe we should commandeer that thing and hit the hills" in a sort of joking way. But not so much joking as Tanner knew too that some of their work was going to be picked apart.

He smiled though when the landing ramp came down and Admiral McQueen walked down the ramp in big strides like he was in a hurry, which Tanner secretly hoped was true. Someone with an eye on their PDA clock seldom dug deep enough to see what lay behind the facade, he knew. *Hardly sounded like the admiral though,* he thought as he too stepped forward to come to attention and snapped a salute at the same time as his boss beside him. An aide had come along too, a CWO of some type, and they weren't introduced to her, but she smiled at them nonetheless.

"At ease, you two," Admiral McQueen said as he too saluted back and then joined them on the tarmac.

"This will be a formal inspection—you both know that. But I'm also aware that the almost insurmountable list of items that you two have faced and tried to get done is something that will mitigate circumstances. That said, safety and usability are the most important items, I would think, for opening day in, what, thirty-two days, I figure. I don't care if networks aren't up or if students are sitting on boxes—as long as we can get the new semester started is what I'm here to discover," he said as he began walking away from the *Tripp* and toward a flyer that lay on the next pad.

"Sir," Admiral Higgins said as they strode alongside Admiral McQueen, "we've done our best with what we had to work with. And yes, as far as we can tell, the new semester will begin on time. Some boxes will also be in use, but on the whole, the Academy Towers are ready to open on the deadline," he finished off.

Tanner nodded and hoped that the admiral didn't get up to see Tower Number One and the horrible mistakes that had been made in the residences area nor Tower Number Three and the issues still that were arising as the quartermaster could be heard yelling about lateness all the way out to the flyer parking area. *Still, we did get much done over the past ninety days*, he thought and then took a rear seat as the two admirals took first row seats and Higgins nodded to the pilot. The aide sat one more row back in the flyer and looked out the window like the rest of them.

The flyer lifted off, circled first, and then picked up speed as it turned to head out for the canyons where the new Academy Towers were located. Tanner couldn't hear the talk between the two admirals, as the interior of the flyer was noisy, and that was a good thing, he thought. No sense in listening in on that which he couldn't change, he figured, and he settled back for the quick flight.

The pilot was good, and he came down the canyon and spun around all four towers to do a full circle and then lit down on Tower Number One perfectly too. Having two admirals as passengers made a pilot pay particular attention to his craft and that thought had just been borne out for sure.

As the three of them left the flyer, the aide tagged along too, and moments later, they were climbing the bank of stairs up to the massive double doors that lofted well above them.

"If all the towers used this kind of architecture, then any visitor will be impressed," Admiral McQueen said. His head tilted back and swung from side to side, as he looked around. It was an entrance made to impress. It made what one could find inside currently not quite as spectacular. *"At least not yet,"* Tanner said to himself, and as they went through the spacious lobby area, he could see there were still issues with equipment, furniture movements, and installations.

Ahead were more than twenty or so dollies, all carrying cased goods like desks to be moved up via the elevators onto their assigned floors and residence rooms, where students, interns, and even professional installers were to put them together and install them.

Except, of course, there were issues—like the elevator clerk ahead who was checking, then checking again and then checking a third time, the cases on the next two dollies that were to go up.

Tanner picked now to try to help, and in one of his best helpful voices, he asked the clerk what the problem was, and he got a frustrated look back from the man.

"Sir, next dolly says this equipment—two desks, two cabinets, two bookcases, and two mobile chairs —is going to room T1-2812. But Sir, the next dolly has the exact same case delivery specs too. And it's a plain double room, Sir—no way for all this to fit in one double. So someone has mislabeled the cases, Sir," he said, and as Tanner double-checked, he saw the man was right.

"Easy one to handle. Send both up to floor

twenty-eight, have one only delivered to the proper room—twenty-eight twelve, I believe? Have the other offloaded by the elevators in a stack so the specs can still be seen. Something tells me that when the twenty-eighth floor is complete, there'll be one residence double room with nothing in same— use this cached set there. Got it?" he asked nicely.

The clerk nodded and got the dolly students to repeat that back to him as the admirals and Tanner walked on.

"If that's the kind of issues that we're facing and answers seem to be so easy, I can smile a bit more about the deadline opening day event," Admiral McQueen said dryly as they went all the way across the big foyer to the reception area.

A round of salutes and at eases followed as the admiral asked questions of the staff behind the reception desk.

Most of the answers were fine. Not a single person mentioned the plumbing issues up on floor forty-one, and nobody mentioned the utility corridor issues on the top two floors either. Tower Number One was supposed to hold residences, retail floors of stores for student purchases, academy issuing of quartermaster items like uniforms, and lastly utility services like laundry and cleaning.

Most, Tanner knew, *had gone well. Except for those*

plumbing issues. But it seemed like the admiral didn't much want to leave the lobby, so they'd escape that one.

Nodding and then asking a couple more questions—based Tanner could tell on the reception desk's knowledge of issues around the move in of the students themselves—Admiral McQueen seemed to have reached an end to his questions and turned to look at Admiral Higgins.

"Fine, let's get on to Tower Number Two," he said, as he strode away from the reception desk and toward the big open doorway.

As he walked, he dictated to his aide, and Tanner was pleased to note that the tower with the biggest issues had escaped closer scrutiny—at least so far.

It was the same for the rest of the towers too. Tower Number Two with the classrooms, study hall, professors' lounges, offices, and lecture theaters too all had issues as well, but for the most part were in good order.

The admiral, again, never left the lobby but did make a note to his aide that he'd checked the issue that he had listed where more than fifty different professors had all complained bitterly about poor construction management. He noted with a tip of his head to Higgins that satisfying the hundreds of professors was a job that just couldn't be done for one and all. Yet, he had her write down the job was in hand and that he was happy with the solutions that had been found.

Tanner, of course, didn't catch the admiral's eye over that one; *it had been his own ignoring of those hundreds and hundreds of messages about wrong colored carpet and white boards that were blue and that a custom desk wouldn't fit within an alcove. He knew he'd answer for same one day, but it appeared to not be today.*

At Tower Number Three, the quartermaster was a happy camper today. Rear Admiral Higgins had okayed, just three days ago, the advancement of funds to allow the bureaucrat to spend, spend, spend, and the smile on his face boded well. Admiral McQueen noted the change in the man who'd only last week threatened to quit the RIM Navy if something wasn't done. Now, he held up a sweatshirt in academy colors with the logo of the academy and the new four towers added too. He was proud of his swag, and the admiral mentioned that he'd love one and one for his aide too, and they were quickly passed over.

The flight over to Tower Number Four was a short one too, and in that lobby again, there were lengthy lines of fixtures and equipment being taken up to various floors. Admiral McQueen did his due diligence on this one, Tanner noted. He took the time to speak to some of the students who were manhandling those dollies to find out how they were instructed and where their supervisors were at that moment. Some, of course, were ten feet away and almost tripped over themselves to get in front of him to answer his queries.

Not that there was much to say. Dollies with loads came in off the landing levels and were moved up via elevators. Then each dolly team took same to its designated floor and room. Sometimes, they then needed to unload and assemble the items, but other times, a team of installers awaited the next round of equipment.

The admiral nodded. "Looks good here too," he said as he looked around and then went off to the academy registrar's offices ahead. He looked around, as Tanner watched, and he commented some things to his aide who typed them into her tablet. He went from there to the administration offices too and found, as Tanner knew he would, dozens of clerks and filing going on. Humongous bins of records and paper files were being slowly re-filed inside new cabinets in new locations and sub-offices too.

Tanner smiled. *You'd think that paper files and the actual filing and storage of same would have been dead for a thousand years. Not so, he knew. Paper still ruled … as a hard copy carried so much more weight when referred to than a line on a tablet screen.*

Higgins commented on something about the carpet coming a bit later as they were standing on a bare sub-floor in the administration offices, and the aide made a note of that too, Tanner saw.

And they were done, and Tanner thought *that both he and Higgins breathed the same sigh of relief.*

On the way back in the flyer, McQueen asked for one full circle of the four towers, and as the pilot complied, he half-turned to face Tanner a row behind as well as Higgins who was sitting beside him.

"Report will be satisfactory, for your information. I am happy with what I saw and will report back on same to the RIM Executive Council too at our next meeting. I have meetings tomorrow with the Master Adept out at her location, and I will be back on the *Tripp* to go to Juno tomorrow by noon. If you've anything else—let me know by then. And if you can stop the flow of the hundreds of messages from administrators and professors who all claim that you're ignoring their small requests for changes-do so and do so now. I hear that some of these messages are even getting sent to heads of state to remind them that their next batch of grads might not be up to snuff because a white board was white instead of blue. Good gosh. Stop them if you can—get them handled, I mean. Oh, and I don't need to know about the plumbing issues in Tower Number One either, I know you're on top of same," he added dryly.

Figures, Tanner thought, *that he'd know but not dig any deeper on site. We've got to get those new lines, vents and drains installed STAT.* He nodded just like Admiral Higgins did.

Moments later, the circle around the last tower done, the flyer headed back to Dessau and the naval base.

#####

Seems like it's admiral's week, Tanner thought as he waited once again with Admiral Higgins as the flyer touched down on the Tower Number Four landing tarmac and spun to a stop. Moments later, Admiral Childs, the head of the academy, jumped down and strode over to meet them, *and that stride,* Tanner thought, *looked a bit ominous.*

Admiral Childs had been the head of the RIM Confederacy Navy for over twenty years, and he had been moved over to run the academy when Admiral McQueen had been appointed. If anyone knew the RIM Navy, it was Childs, and as he'd been the head of the academy now for over five years, he knew it well too.

It had been Childs whom Tanner had approached back a few years to help plan a pseudo-mutiny of cadets so that the Pirates could be tracked, followed, and engaged. The plan had worked, which Tanner knew was a good thing or else he'd have still been in a brig somewhere over on Halberd, the RIM Confederacy prison planet. Childs had kept their plan close to his vest too— he'd not told Admiral McQueen about it and had followed through on his own. *Able navy man,* Tanner thought, as he put a smile on his face.

"Wipe that smile off, Captain!" Childs drilled at him. "Do you have any idea as to the number of complaints that I have on my console about you and your inability to get things done with the tower construction issues, Captain?" he asked, but Tanner knew he didn't want an answer.

He wiped the smile off his face as the two admirals shook hands. He snapped a salute up and held it as the admiral took his time before he saluted back.

"Sir, sorry about that—it's just that—"

"I know perfectly well what it's like to have dozens and dozens of requests for hundreds of changes—they used to infect my own inbox—now they go to you," he said and smiled.

Admiral Childs nodded then and held out his hand. "Not to worry, Captain, I'm so very glad that you are the buffer tween me and my professors and the quartermaster and the registrar and the principal and the whole admin staff. So nice to have an inbox without their constant complaints about the color of this and the nap on the carpet and the missing crown moldings in the washrooms. So nice indeed," he said, and both of the admirals chuckled.

"So, let's go in and remember to look interested, take notes where needed on your PDAs, and yes, we'll be going up to visit some of the major issues here in Tower Number Four. With me," he said, and he turned to walk toward the massive wide-open double doors of the tower itself.

While Childs was a rear admiral, exactly the same rank as Rear Admiral Higgins, he took the lead and was followed by Higgins on this tour, Tanner noted. They moved off the landing tarmac lot, got the nod from a Provost guard at the gateway, and then mounted the long set of stairs up to the ground floor entrance.

Once inside, they went directly across the large foyer and past the reception desk area to the administration offices. Admiral Childs was not stopped by a soul on his way inside. They made a turn or two, missing the registrar's offices by taking a back corridor that Tanner had never been in before to a plain door halfway down the hall. Childs slapped his hand on the ID plate at the side of the door frame, which opened it, he and walked in with Higgins and Tanner behind him.

Surprising the man seated at the large desk in this well-furnished office was one thing.

Surprising him as he had his feet up on the corner of his desk as he was talking via Ansible to someone on the screen that sat on the far wall was too much for him—he swung his feet down and hit the pause button on his console.

"Sir—Admiral Childs, Admiral Higgins ... and Captain ... what a surprise to have you ... drop in ... so to speak," he said, and the stammer was a bit noticeable.

"Principal Boulos, so nice to see you again," Childs said as he dragged a chair over to sit in front of the desk and nodded for the rest of them to do the same.

"Remind me, Boulos, what it is you do here— what a principal of a university does, I mean?" he asked dryly.

Ekram Boulos nodded. His longish salt and pepper hair drooped over one half of his forehead, and he swept that back with a well-manicured hand. A Caliphate alien, he was unusual looking in that he did not dress his six-foot-five-inch frame with the usual Caliphate citizen clothing. Instead, he favored the more normal business attire of humans. His dress was immaculate, Tanner thought. He wore a perfectly pressed light blue shirt with some kind of a swath of color around the neck and highly polished boots into which were tucked amber pants. On the far chair, his amber jacket had been neatly folded and placed there while he worked at his desk.

"I look after all of the things that you—the academy headmaster—does not. Which means that I look after the hiring of staff members, communicating with the RIM Confederacy members, planning our academic calendars and the like. Well, in fact, you do all of those items, yes, but it usually falls to me to look after all of the smaller details of same, Sir," he said, and his voice was trying to please.

Childs nodded. "And in this special case where we have construction on four brand new towers with all of those issues, what were you to do to aid in same?" he asked.

Boulos sat up a bit straighter and shuffled his feet under his desk a couple of times, looking down at his console while trying to come up with an answer. It appeared he failed at that, as after a moment, he held up both hands, palms up, shrugged, and said, "Why, I didn't have any input at all, Admiral."

Childs nodded. "You do as of right now, Principal Boulos. I want—Captain, send off all of those personal requests for changes to our principal —all of them, mind you. I want you, Boulos, to look after every single one, personally. No aides, no assistants at all. You are to work with whomever has requested changes to get it done. I want happy,

happy administrators and professors on the academy grounds when the new semester starts— got that, Principal Boulos?" he said, his voice strong and demanding.

Boulos nodded and nodded again. "Absolutely, Admiral—I'll look after them all ... how many could there be even," he said with a half-smile.

Tanner spoke up then and said, "Since I got here, about three hundred or so."

That wiped the smile off the Principal's face. He squirmed a bit as the size of the new task settled on his shoulders, but he said not a single word.

"Fine. By the start of the new semester then, Principal Boulos," Admiral Childs said, and he got up and led the way out the back door to the office and back to the foyer of Tower Number Four.

Once there, they waited for an up elevator amid the rows of equipment-laden dollies, and he looked over at Admiral Higgins.

"That man was sent to us by the Caliph himself as one of the best administrators available, but I'm having my doubts," he said, and he shook his head as they got on the elevator and were still able to cram in two more dollies too.

Up they went first to floor eighteen, and one dolly left there. Then up to floor twenty-seven for the last dolly where they all got out.

Admiral Higgins took the lead and led them

around the floor as this one was housing offices for deans, chairmen, and coordinators. There were some utility issues still in one corridor as the floor tiles hadn't been laid as yet, and Tanner made a note of that on his PDA. Childs nodded and walked, and he asked few questions. In a short time, they were back at the elevator and then headed down to the ground floor.

Once there, Childs again led the way directly across from the elevators to the large wall that faced it and stood there for a full minute staring at it. Once or twice, he turned his head to look to his left at the big open doors and then to his right to the reception desk area too.

"Here, I think is the spot. Been looking for a bit to see where it should go, and this is about the best spot I can think of," he said.

"Sir? What should be here?" Admiral Higgins questioned.

"Our Academy Alumni of Valor Memorial, Admiral Higgins. Where we show the photos and name badges and ranks of all academy alumni who have died as RIM Navy officers and non-commissioned navy men. We put up their pictures and a small plaque too with a short bio and list the event that took their lives too. It will go here—Captain, arrange for it to be moved from the old academy grounds over to be here—and it must look sharp too, Captain. Blue and gold and the dagger must also show—well, you know what I mean as I remember that you were on the *RN Kerry*, Captain, and you've seen same. Done before the new semester starts too, Captain," he finished off, and without a further word, he turned and marched out of the spacious lobby to return to his flyer.

"Went better than I'd expected," Admiral Higgins said as he and Tanner left the tower too to go back to Dessau and their offices in the administration area of the naval base there.

"Don't think that the principal will get much done though," Tanner said, and that got a resounding snort from Higgins as they went back to work.

David just sat there and didn't say a thing.

The fact that he'd lost his own mother seven years ago was one thing.

Now, Kendal had just explained to him that he'd lost another family member—Aunt Mariam too.

Lost but not really. She'd tried to soften the blow and then it had all come out.

She had to explain about the Inner Circle and her own mother's involvement with it decades ago. She'd had to explain how way back when she and Mariam had been just conceived, that the process of culling the set of twins into one superior Issian and one that in fact would be stillborn was a new procedure. That somehow a mistake had been made, and while she was the superior one, Mariam had still been born. But Mariam had lain in restraints for more than thirty years. Yet she could still mind link with Kendal, and that was such a hard thing to experience because while for her it freed her of the horrors of being a captive in the MedWards—for Kendal it made her that captive. She felt what Mariam felt. She knew what it was like as their minds engaged and she cried and spasmed over and over.

He had listened.

He had asked few questions.

He had wondered *why they hadn't just killed Mariam—an answer she did not have.*

But then he'd gotten up and moved away from his chair at his net console and went to the rear-facing window. From here, one couldn't see the dome, as it lay directly in front of the house, but only the whole of Aporia, as it stretched out to the far side of the city. He stared at the city skyline, nodded a couple of times, then came back to sit down once again, and looked at her.

"Aunt Kendal—I am so sorry about your twin. I had no idea, of course … and my mom never mentioned her either. That all said, I know it must

be tough on you—but what I want to know is—
why are you telling me this now?"

Smart boy, she thought, and she looked down at
her palms. They were so dry usually, but now she
could see the sheen of perspiration.

"I need your techie skills, David. I know that you
were once a great leader over at the academy in
their IT division, and I'm hoping that you can help
me somewhat," she said.

"What do you need, Aunt Kendal," he said.

She explained that she was allowed only one trip
a year into the MedWard to see Mariam. That she
was never allowed in the room—actually on the
secure wing itself. She saw her only through a side
window, and it hurt her so much to see her twin
imprisoned that she'd forgone some of her yearly
visits. Too often. Too many times.

But she also knew that as she'd looked around the
whole patient room, anywhere but at the thrashing
twin tied to the bed, that there were cameras there.
Many cameras.

So security—maybe via AI—she didn't know,
was high.

But there would be archived footage of same.

And she wanted some of that for her use.

When David nodded, she thought that was easy,
but then he asked more.

"And when you've gotten these tapes, what are

you going to do with them, Aunt Kendal?"

She looked away for a moment over at the walls of his room. He had played pretty good rugby in high school, she remembered. She'd driven him to games and practices, and in his senior year, the team had made the RIM Planetary finals. That they'd lost to some other planet was long gone ... but the smiles on this nephew's face were what was important. On the wall was a big poster that one of the parents on the team had made, and a younger David smiled back at her, wearing his red-and-white-striped rugger shirt. Days gone by ... and she shook her thoughts back to the present.

"I intend to make them public so that the city council knows what is going on right here in Aporia. So that the citizens of Eons learn what our Inner Circle is up to as well. I intend to become—what's the phrase—a whistle-blower!"

She looked at him and then pointed to the console screen in front of him.

"Can you do this—this hack, is it called—and not get caught?"

He nodded. *Years back as a part of the program team he'd led, their group had done things like this as a part of competitions. Only competitions had often been challenges to find a way in to various Eons systems, institutions, and businesses too. While he'd not bothered with the MedWards, he knew a fellow who had, and he might still have an archive of that month's messages and examples. Otherwise, he knew whom to message.*

"I can. It will take a bit, but yes, I can download much vid footage, and then you'd need to see what parts you want to use, and I can then turn it into a working vid for you. But Aunt Kendal, I wouldn't think our local city council gives a crap about this stuff ..." he said, and she could hear the plain truth in what he said.

She nodded but then held up a finger. "Except that I know that in a couple of months, the MedWard expansion funding is coming to the council for their verifications—so I've already registered as an interested party and a speaker on behalf of my Twins Cooperative storefront business. I need that video in that kind of time—we okay with that?"

He nodded. "No problem, Aunt Kendal—one more thought, will I ever get to meet Aunt Mariam?"

She shrugged and a tear came to her eye. "I do not know, David ... but if I can, then yes ... yes, indeed!"

He smiled at her and said, "Just like meeting you, right?"

That made her cringe inside, but she smiled back at him.

When he sees the video footage, he'll know better.

She got up and went back to her kitchen to work on her speech to be used in a few months' time.

CHAPTER SIX

As he applied CPR to the young man's chest, Tanner thought *that no one could have seen this coming.*

He took a second to push the cadet's head a little straighter to make sure the airway wasn't clogged.

Blood bubbles were forming on his chest, where something had pierced his lung, and the resulting air that Tanner was blowing into the young man was coming back out.

He kept it up—he'd been working on this one for over five minutes, and the EMTs from Dessau were just now flying in. He continued to pump the chest to try to circulate the blood, thirty compressions at a time. Then back to doing the two big rescue breaths and then thirty more chest compressions.

He looked up as a pair of shoes suddenly

appeared in front of him, squishing the broken green flyer windshield glass, and found an EMT looking down at him.

"Sir, quick triage and I'd like to get in there, okay by you?" the tech said.

Tanner nodded, carefully got up, and tried to avoid the broken hulk of the flyer that he'd been able to crawl into to drag the cadet half-clear.

He caught his arm on a splinter of metal that was the flyer doorway frame, and it cut him slightly, but that was the least of his worries as he surveyed the damage and mayhem around him.

The EMT looked up and said, "Thanks for your help, Captain, this one is gonna make it, I think."

Tanner nodded back and looked around.

From where he stood, he could see that the automatic AI built into Tower Number One had been called to duty as huge hoses still poured foam and water onto the floor where a teal blue flyer jutted out after crashing directly into the tower around floor seven. Four more lay in wreckage now around him, and he pushed away from the one he'd been able to help on. He noted one still burned.

He looked over at the cadets who were milling around those flyers and yelled at them all. "Someone get into the tower and go to the utility corridor at the back end and get some fire extinguishers out here STAT."

He was pleased to see that almost ten of them ran off quickly to follow his orders. He rubbed the blood away from his uniform sleeve and strode up to the balance of the cadets.

"All of you—there's going to be a full investigation into this—but can anyone offer up what they saw? How'n the hell did this happen?" he said, and his voice was like a blow.

Most of them snapped to attention but not all, he noted, as he said, "As you were," and the one who seemed to be off to one side pushed through others to stand before him.

"Sir, I have no idea why this happened, nor do I know who any of the cadets are. But I was stopped by the Provost guard at the gate here, as it seems there was an issue with my ID card.

"While he was messaging someone, I could hear all of a sudden the noise from a whole group more'n a dozen I'd say, Sir, flyers all come screaming around the tower—like they were racing, Sir. I do not know if that was true, but they did at least two more laps around the tower, 'til someone in that bright yellow one," he said as he pointed to the still burning flyer hulk thirty yards away, "cut off the one that hit the tower itself. That made the yellow one yaw badly to starboard, and it took down all the rest of these ones, Sir," he said.

No one spoke.

Tanner didn't know if what he had just been told was true, as he'd been inside coming down the elevators when the flyer had hit the tower, and that had stopped the elevators. He'd been able to force the door open, climb down to floor five, and then run down the last few flights to get out of the building. Once outside, he saw that cadet trying to get out of his green flyer, and he'd run to give CPR.

Tanner didn't also know if this student cadet had just done something right or wrong either. There was certainly nothing wrong in telling the truth, but then again, perhaps among students was a code of silence that might have ruled on this kind of storytelling. He didn't know, but a look at all the other cadet faces showed him that the cadet who told had done the right thing.

At least he said what he saw.

And the fact that student cadets were racing their flyers was also surely not a new thing either—but the accident surely was.

He nodded. "And your name, Cadet, is?" he asked politely, turning on his PDA which was missed by no one standing there.

"Cadet Herbert Fleen, Sir. Of the Duchy d'Avigdor, Sir. Third year cadet graduate, going into my final senior year, Sir," the cadet barked out.

Tanner nodded. "Right, all present will be my own crime scene party. Ten of you, please form a perimeter around the crashed flyers, and allow NO

ONE to enter the areas except for Provost guards or EMTs. I am Captain Tanner Scott—2IC here at the towers, so my word is law. Anyone has any questions, you send them to me. Ten more of you, I want you to report to that Provost—uh—Provost corporal over there, and tell him you're assigned to help him with whatever might need to be done. You, you, and you," he said as he pointed at Cadet Fleen and two more, "you belong to me, follow closely—record all on your PDAs too, that's an order for you all," he said as he turned and strode away to enter the tower.

At the doorway, a Provost guard attempted to stop him, but with a pointed look at the guard, he backed off immediately, saluted, and said, "Yes, Sir, no problems here, Sir," over and over.

Tanner went straight through the lobby that still had students, retail store personnel, and staff pouring out of the stairs and racing out of the building.

He turned to the long corridor that went past the reception desk area and then took the first doorway to the left. Next was a jog down that short hallway to an unmarked door on the left side again, right up tight to the west wall of the tower.

Opening it by jamming his palm against the security plate on the door frame, he went up the stairs that were empty of anyone else, and he took the stairs two at a time. Below, he could hear his three cadets struggling to keep up but he didn't slow until he reached the sixth floor, and he went out the door at a fly. He raced down the utility corridor once more, making his way to where the flyer might have hit and found he was a floor—at least a floor—short.

He went back to the private stairs and up one more floor, his cadets now almost able to keep up.

Again, out the stairwell door and ahead of him after the first left-hand corner, he could see Provost guards, students, and some laundry staff all milling about.

He barked "Coming through" at them all, and they moved aside clumsily, but he was able to force his way through them all to get to the doorway that still had small billows of smoke wafting through it. He could hear the AI running the sprinklers and even directing the hosed extensions as he had to squat to look in any farther. He said "Wait" to his cadets as he edged in and found his way blocked by what looked like the aluminum wall frames and twisted shards of this residence room—desks, beds, and even some plumbing lines too. The smoke was coming from the flyer, and he dropped to his knees to slowly crawl over those metal frames and found himself at the rear end of a Provost sergeant who was backing out of the room.

He tapped the man on his back and the Provost half-turned toward him.

"Sergeant, what about the cadet?" he asked plainly.

The Provost sergeant shook his head. "Sir, the flyer twisted before impact—the side that the cadet was on hit first, and I'm afraid the impact alone would have killed him—or the resulting fire that the AI only now is getting under control. He's gone, Sir, I'm afraid." His tone was one of sadness.

Tanner nodded, clasped the guard for a second on his arm, and then he too backed up and out of the room.

Moments later, the Provost sergeant stood up beside him and rubbed his face, still coved with soot from the room's fire.

"So sorry, Sir … surely this could have been avoided," he said as he pushed past Tanner to get out of the mass of people.

Tanner motioned for his cadets and outlined their jobs. In less than two minutes, all the rubberneckers were gone, and the area was clean of all except for a couple of Provost guards positioned at the residence room doorway and the EMT who also had come back out of the room.

He took off his short mask, wiped his forehead, and looked at Tanner.

"Sir, that one is gone. We'll await the settling of

the fire routines, the Provost guards, and I'd expect someone from the local Dessau Police force too—but once they're all done, we'll remove the remains, Sir," he said with respect.

Tanner nodded.

He'd have to call Rear Admiral Higgins immediately as he and Admiral McQueen were over at the Issian walled city in a meeting with the Master Adept.

He'd have to get the EMTs to identify the body so he could notify the boy's next of kin.

He'd have to get the body properly looked after, and he'd have to find out how to do that—maybe the admiral's aide, Lieutenant CoSharan could help with that one.

He'd have to get statement interview times coordinated with the Dessau Police so that each could help with their case.

And lastly, he'd have to see if he could get this all done with a minimum of notice by the rest of the RIM Confederacy ... the big opening day was less than four weeks away, and this kind of an accident did not bode well for the new academy.

Accident. Yes, this had been an accident—and not a stupid cadet race.

That's the card to play, he thought.

#####

About ninety lights outward off Lambda4, the *SN Majestic* was in trouble.

The huge liner, with its hundreds of passengers and sleepers too, had been on this run from Lambda4 to Juno in the RIM Confederacy for more than a hundred years. Seenra-made, she ran at two lights a day, and for the most part, the daily monitoring of gauges and displays was the only thing that ever happened on board.

Like all the previous cruises outward from the center to the fringes of the galaxy, the *Majestic* was following her normal course. She turned the twenty-six degrees to port when they hit the seventy-four lights out of her last port to avoid the huge nebula ahead, and this time she had done so perfectly, as always.

The thing was, this reflection-class nebula was not something that could be counted on to stay put, year after year, as it swirled and slowly gave up its path to local gravity wells. This was something to not worry about, as most nebulas were simply huge gaseous swirls of color—most but not all. Some, like the one that now surrounded the *Majestic*, were also carriers of particulate materials—dust, as the reflection nebula around them reflected local star shine in its normal bright neon blue colorations.

This nebula had changed its course, for whatever reason, and the *Majestic* had cruised right into a gigantic lobe of the bright blue layers of dust and gas. Not a problem, normally, as there really was nothing inside the fog to hit; it was only a problem for the navigation AI and its supporting Ansible navigation controls, as the alarms began to chirrup up on the bridge monitors.

A crewman put down his vid player and listened to the bleating of the alarm for a moment before telling the AI that he had it.

He got up and went over to the NAV console, and as he was the only one on the bridge for this shift, he sat and looked down at the monitor.

The *Majestic* had inadvertently run straight into the massive blue arm of the nebula and was flying blind, but all the gauges read that the ship was fine. On course. On time. "No other items to worry about," he said to himself, as he killed the flashing AI alarm on his screen and then looked out the front view-screen.

"Go to infrared," he said to the AI, and the screen changed from the fog of blue to the normal star field that lay ahead. He keyed in the map function and again got a verification that the ship was on its true course.

"Run from J to Z band, three seconds each, on screen," he then told the AI, and as he watched, the infrared display changed but didn't change at all. Not a thing ahead in the fog. Distant stars of the

RIM only far, far ahead.

He nodded.

He made notes in his log and filed that away in the pass-along log that the next shift would read when they came on duty.

What he didn't know to check on was the ionization of the dust that the *Majestic* was now flying through at two lights a day.

It collected slowly on many of the instruments and various arrays on the ship and began to thinly coat them.

He didn't know that as this lobe of the nebula was almost five lights thick, that the Majestic would be coating its arrays for a couple of days.

He didn't know that this could cause a problem with the NAV AI as it asked the Ansible navigation for positional readings hundreds of times a minute.

He didn't know that the *Majestic* would follow those headings incrementally and move the helm by thousandths of a degree each time it polled the Ansible for location readings.

He just didn't know …

And he returned to his comfortable seat and the vid he'd been watching.

#####

"Sit, please, all of you," Admiral Higgins said to

the nine cadets who'd filed into the administration conference room and then had snapped to attention, saluting as they stared straight ahead.

They did just that, Tanner noted, and he was looking them over when the admiral began to lambaste them all.

"You idiots! You stupid, stupid idiots. Did you not think that having a race around a tower might lead to an accident? And I'm calling it an accident as yet we have no eyewitnesses who can swear that one or more of you pushed Cadet—" he stopped and looked at Tanner.

"Cadet Minden, Sir, one Jeremy Minden of the Abstract realm, Sir," he barked out, identifying the casualty.

The admiral nodded and continued Yes, Cadet Minden may have been forced into the tower. We don't know, but if we do find that, the guilty party or parties here in this room will spend decades out on Halberd, the RIM prison planet."

He threw his stylus onto the tablet in front of him, and the whole room knew he was pissed.

"Explanations, please? Can someone tell me how this happened? Why this happened? What the reasons were for this race?"

The cadets sat still. Tanner looked over at one of them—he didn't have the cadet's name, so he just pointed at him.

"Cadet, I don't know if you know, but I was the one who gave you CPR after your flyer slammed into the tarmac. EMTs really did the work of saving your life though—so can you tell me anything at all?"

He asked, knowing that the young man would feel some kind of responsibility. Hopefully as he'd been the one that had dragged him out of the ruined flyer and supported his life until the EMTs had arrived, that kind of liability could be used.

The cadet shuffled in his seat, and his eyes never left the table in front of him as he ran a hand back through his hair but didn't speak yet.

As Tanner got the cadet's ID from his tablet, it told him that this human was from Hope, a RIM Confederacy planet, and had been at the academy for two years so far—he was going into his junior year.

Name is Mano Berrak, it appeared. Hope, Tanner thought, is that planet where due to its huge, huge oceans, most of the landmasses were smaller islands and small sub-sub-continents. As he'd learned before, that had turned their society into small independent groups of very individualized persons, each with their own way of doing things. That might work here, he thought.

"Can you not offer up anything, Cadet Berrak?" he said in the midst of the silence around the room.

The cadet finally nodded his head. "Sir, yes Sir. We were all coming in from Dessau—I don't know how many of us there were, but a few of us pushed past the norms of flyer usage, Sir. We—and yes, I was one of them—flew down deep into the canyon, buzzed the river and a couple of boats on same. We angled up via some of the canyon mesas, and all of a sudden, it was a race, Sir. Some flyers are quicker than others, yet all are limited by the skill of the flyer pilot. We raced back up the canyon to the mountains—then did a full loop around same and then back to Tower Number One," he said and then he paused.

Another cadet interrupted.

"Sir, Cadet Williams here, Sir. I was in the lead, and I took it on myself to do a quick run to the last tower, Tower Number Four, then a loop back all the way to Tower Number One. It was there that I'd suppose that Cadet Minden's flyer hit the tower, Sir. I was in the lead so I didn't see it—but it was an accident, Sir. Not a single cadet would ever force another to crash, Sir. That I do know."

Skoggian, so his purple skin was shiny still with youth, Tanner saw. He had leaned forward to speak, and his hands were folded carefully in front of him. He looked like he said what he thought was true—and suddenly Tanner wished Bram could have been with them. Having an Issian Adept at the table would have helped, and he made a mental note to ask for that later from the admiral.

He nodded. "Does anyone have anything else to say? It was an accident—Minden just didn't make the turn with enough space between his flyer and the wall of the tower—hence the accident? Is that your story," he asked yet again.

All the cadet heads in front of him were nodding.

Cadet Berrak offered up one more thing. "Sir, as we were going into that final loop around the tower, all I know is that Minden was at the tail end —it stands to reason that if he could have cut the corner a little tighter, he might have moved up, Sir …" he said and that too got some nods.

"Fine. I want your written reports in my INBOX by sixteen hundred hours today," the admiral said quietly.

"And I want your solemn promise that your racing days are over, for as long as you're at the academy."

Again, the all the cadets nodded, and after the admiral said, "Dismissed," they got up, saluted, and then left the conference room.

He looked at Tanner. "Comments, Captain?" he asked as he toyed with the stylus on the table, twisting it one way and then the other.

"Sir, all I know is that this Cadet Berrak is from Hope and they tend to be individuals who handle themselves in their own ways. I would think then that he told the truth. Minden was at the end of the line of flyers, tried to cut the corner—Sir, I think we've all tried that in our own past—and cut it too close. I don't think we'll find out much more, Sir," he added.

The admiral nodded and then made some notes on his tablet, the stylus finally being used for what it was made.

"Captain—I'll leave it to you to contact the parents of Cadet Minden—normal sympathies and all. I'd like to put him up on Admiral Child's Wall of Valor too, but leave that one to me. Talk to the academy communications department too, as we need to put out an official notice of the accident as well as a media release too. Get me copies of same before they go live too, please, so I can vet same," he said, and he tossed the stylus one more time at his tablet.

"Goddamn kids. Did they never consider that this kind of thing could happen?" he swore and shook his head.

We've all been young, Tanner thought, *as we seldom get caught doing stupid things ... but hopefully, these cadets had learned ... it surely had cost enough ...*

#####

As the brace of EliteGuards strode into the

conference room in the Dessau landing port administration building, Tanner had a growing suspicion *that something was up.*

"Ten-Shun," the lead guard said, and there was only one reason that a lowly sergeant could ever use that term to the admirals at the table—a Royal was about to enter the room. It wasn't normally done, but this time, for some reason, it was, and as he quickly rose to his feet, only a few seconds behind Admiral Higgins and Childs, he said over and over to himself, "Let it be the Baroness, let it be the Baroness."

When the Lady St. August walked in a minute later, he, like all present, snapped a salute and held it.

She went to the empty chair at the head of the table, held the back in both hands, looked them all over, and then said, "Thank you, one and all" as she twisted the chair to take her seat.

A vision in ultramarine blue, he thought, as he carefully sat down beside Admiral Higgins on one side of the large table and noted everyone else was a bit nonplussed. He looked down at his tablet so he wouldn't have to look at her hair, which was swept off to one side, a blue sapphire the width of a plum holding it there. Her top was some kind of leather but with a scale pattern of an animal he'd never seen before, and it was matched by her knee-high boots that were the same color and scale pattern.

He toyed with his tablet, seemingly to make notes perhaps as Admiral Childs took over the chairing of the meeting and went around the table making introductions.

"Of course, representing the Barony of Neres is our Lady St. August," he began, and she fluttered a wave at the table, as she was staring at no one in particular but looking at each face as they were to be introduced.

"We have Admiral Higgins here," Childs said as he looked across the table and half-pointed to the man.

"He'd be the one who has wrangled the construction so damn—pardon me, My Lady—so darn well that we are going to make our deadlines and open with full occupancy permits in twenty-three days. Ably aided by Captain Tanner Scott," Childs then said as he pointed at Tanner, smiled, and repeated "Ably aided, indeed, Ma'am. Between these two navy men, we're on track—and under budget too, the bean-counters tell us," he said.

She nodded.

That was all that she did, as Childs went on.

"We also have there the top construction bosses led by Superintendent Bill Chapman, the smiling man down the table a bit," he said, and sure enough, the superintendent was smiling.

"So nice to meet you, Ma'am. And as Admiral Childs said, we're right on target to meet the deadline in about three weeks."

"I would hope so, Superintendent—you've been at this for, what, almost a year?" she said dryly, which quieted down the whole meeting.

She's maybe looking for something to rant about maybe, Tanner thought, *so here goes.*

"Ma'am, not to interrupt, but what the superintendent did not say is that with a construction job like this one—four brand new fifty-plus-story towers, built on a canyon yet coming in on time—is a task that yes, a year ago wasn't envisioned as being that difficult. Yet it was. And it was still met by committed, skilled workers who were well led by the superintendent and his crew chiefs too, Ma'am," Tanner said, his voice not overly forceful but still polite.

She looked at Tanner and said nothing.

Those eyes … piercing yet aloof, drilling down yet saying nothing to anyone else who might be watching …

She nodded and then turned back to Childs. "And this cadet accident, Admiral? Can you explain that to me?"

Tanner interrupted again, holding out a hand to the admiral as a gesture.

"Sir, if I might … Ma'am, the accident was just

that. You know that to be accepted at the academy as a navy officer candidate and to work hard for the four years of university training and co-op naval placements is one of the most vied for items on all youngster's wish lists. The fact that we take only the best should be weighed into this argument—that at times, even the best show some pretty young choices, and this accident was just one of those choices.

"The cadets were just racing to blow off some steam—as well as to show who's king of the castle, and none of them really has enough flyer hours to know their craft and its shortcomings. They all made the same mistake, Ma'am—and one of them in trying to catch up to the race leaders made a choice to push his flyer—and it cost him his life," Tanner said as his own voice cracked, and he took a deep breath before he continued.

"We are all saddened by this, Ma'am, and are only too glad that there was only one casualty. The other students still face the Academy Student Honor Tribunal—to be held in the first semester, Ma'am. And while it's little consolation, Admiral Childs has okayed that we put the victim's ID and photo up on the Academy Wall of Valor for all to see—and hopefully, chill the cadets a bit too, Ma'am."

He spoke in a rush, all the words jumbled

together, but what he said did have the navy men at the table nodding.

It had been an accident, and one that no one would forget.

The Lady St. August looked at him and said nothing.

Her eyes looked at his eyes with what he thought was a bit of sadness, and at the corner of his mouth, a teensy smile appeared.

She nodded and said, "Admiral, let's get to the Agenda, shall we?"

The planning of the academy opening event began, and all present had something to offer. To be held in just twenty-four days, it was to occur, it was decided, on the landing tarmac over at Tower Number Four—the administration tower. Plans were made to have the whole tarmac set up to hold about eighteen hundred guests, so seating, refreshments, and catering were also needed. Someone had to figure out how to shuttle the guests from the other three towers, where parking would be established. Someone else had to arrange for cadet tour leaders to be able to take anyone who landed at one of the other towers to get a tour inside that one before getting on the shuttle to take them to Tower Number Four and the event ceremonies. Someone else needed to arrange for the stage, audio-visual details, AI details, and also for any heads of state who'd all been invited, but the question was, how many were coming.

Admiral Higgins' aide, Lieutenant Kelsey CoSharan, took his cue and began the listing of who was invited and had agreed to attend and who had not bothered to reply. As most of the RIM Confederacy members had a stake in the academy, as their own citizens became cadets there, all had been invited, so the list was a bit more than the forty realms in the Confederacy. But only five had replied so far—the Duchy d'Avigdor, the Barony, Eran, the Caliphate, and Alex'n. Of course, as the date was now barely three weeks away, some had waited too long to even be able to make the event, and that had to be taken into account.

"Lieutenant, if you could then pare down the unanswered list to those who could still get to Eons in twenty-three days, how many heads of state could be expected if they all said yes?" Lady St. August asked politely.

Lieutenant CoSharan nodded, then worked on his tablet for a moment, and said, "We could have as many as thirteen, Ma'am."

She nodded and looked at Admiral Childs. "Then let's plan on having the thirteen, Admiral. If they come—we're good; if they don't, we have some extra space on the stage," she said nicely.

Admiral Childs nodded to her and dug his elbow

into his aide's arm beside him.

Tanner was sure this would be looked after too.

"The Master Adept would, of course, be a speaker—was she not able to come to today's meeting?" Lady St. August inquired.

Everyone looked at each other, and no one spoke up until Admiral Higgins offered his own opinion.

"Ma'am, she was invited, but we never heard back on this at all, Ma'am. But I will ensure that the full report of this meeting—with all its decisions—are made available to her soon after—"

"Admiral, if I might," Lady St. August interrupted, "could I perhaps suggest that you hard copy this and have your number two—Captain Scott—take it directly to her as soon as the meeting is adjourned, perhaps? That would show our respect for her too, yes?" she said sweetly.

The admiral didn't miss a beat. "Ma'am, great idea. I'll personally order the captain," he said as he patted Tanner's arm that lay beside him on the table, "to get it to her personally, Ma'am. Great idea, Ma'am."

Tanner said and did nothing.

Going to the Issian walled city wasn't new to him, and the trip by flyer would be a nice change from the added work of the event planning details that would fall to him.

"Other than her then," Lady St. August said, "as

far as I know, I will also speak as will Admiral Childs and the cadet president too—is there anyone else, Admiral, that I didn't know about?"

He shook his head, but then a thought occurred to him. "Ma'am, as all of the Confederacy realms use the academy, might the other heads of state coming also want a few minutes too, to say offer their congratulations, maybe?" he asked.

She tilted her head to the side, thought on that, then turned back to Lieutenant CoSharan, and said, "Can you check on that too, for us, Lieutenant? It would be better to know up front than have our Master of Ceremonies have to make changes on the fly," she said, as she pushed back her chair and began to rise.

"Exactly who might that be, Ma'am?" Lieutenant CoSharan asked, and Tanner wasn't surprised. Faraway citizens liked all their i's dotted and their T's crossed too.

"Under discussion right now, I understand—I only got the nod to represent the Barony recently—my stepmother, the Baroness, had planned on doing this herself, but there are some issues, I understand, with a newly annexed planet of ours, so she had to go to Ghayth in a hurry," she said.

Ghayth? Issues? Tanner thought—*wondering if Major Stal was there and what could arise that he couldn't handle.*

He was about to inquire right here in the meeting and then caught himself. It wasn't the time nor place.

The Lady St. August rose as her EliteGuards stepped forward and escorted her out of the conference room and out to the Sterling, her frigate in the Barony Navy fleet. She walked, Tanner thought, with grace, but there was a very definite sexy sway to her hips, he also thought as she ambled to the doorway and turned to leave.

Tanner sat, nodded, and listened to the various talk around the table, but he didn't remember much. He did know to tell the speaker "Yes, got it —but message me the details," as he wondered what this was really all about.

CHAPTER SEVEN

As he sat and awaited the Master Adept, Tanner
was sure this whole trip to deliver the minutes of
the academy opening event was just a waste of time.
He had twiddled his thumbs now for more than
twenty minutes, watching the door, but no one had
appeared yet as he sat on the small brown sofa.
Everything here is a shade of brown, he thought.
*Mud brown, cow brown, coffee brown, mocha brown …
no more names for shades of brown. Probably a good
thing,* he thought, as he got up to stretch his legs.
He walked over to the close window on the near
wall and looked out at the landscape beyond the
walled city. As the tower he was in was taller than
those walls, he could see the farms—or what had
been farms at one time—that stretched out toward
the horizon and the mountains on the far horizon.

The farm had surely seen better times as the house was boarded up. The barns were too, and the undergrowth in the fields was surely not from crops.

From behind him came a voice.

"Captain, do you have any idea how long that farm has lain like that, broken and unused?" the Master Adept said, as she glided up beside him in front of the large window.

He couldn't answer, as he had no idea.

She nodded. "More than fifty years, Captain. I've been right here to watch that farm have bumper crops … and now sit fallow in the heavy radiation that has changed our climate. I've watched rain come down so hard that the little slope there," she said as she pointed to the spot where one of the barns lay, "looked like a waterfall. It's not rained here in those decades other than the few showers we get in the spring. Our climate—Eons, in fact—is in jeopardy, Captain, which is why you're here," she said with a degree of justification in her voice.

He turned to look at her as his head tilted to one side, and he pointed back at the coffee table in front of the sofa he'd been sitting on moments earlier.

"Ma'am, I was sent to deliver those," he said, referring to the large envelope that lay there, "as they are the minutes of the academy opening event planning session we just had this morning, Ma'am."

She shook her head as she turned and went to sit on the facing sofa as he took his original seat opposite her.

"Captain, yes, thank you for the report. But that's not why I asked the Lady St. August to request that you be sent to me. This is not at all about that event, Captain—but about you and the lady and Eons too," she said, and Tanner thought she was being a bit odd, but he nodded. And waited.

She took her time before continuing and picked up the tea that was set for her, took a small sip, and then put the cup back carefully on the saucer that was on the table. She brushed her lips with a corner of the napkin she had laying in her lap and she sighed.

"Captain—has it not occurred to you that something else is at work here? That you are so often at the source of things that happen here on the RIM? And yes, while that may be just serendipity rearing its chance head, there are times when we Issians see that you are the crux often of the foreshadowing of those circumstances, Captain. Do you ever feel like that?"

He looked at her and half-smiled.

"Sometimes, Master, I thought that it was because I had a load on—Scotch, I mean, that these things cropped up. But then other times, I felt like if it wasn't me—it'd just be someone else. I'm far from

189

being special in any way, any navy man with my experience would find himself in the same circumstances, and would react the same way. Pull a trigger or turn to port or ask, huh? We think alike, so no, I don't think that I'm special at all, Master," he said, and he knew he'd just spoken the truth for himself.

She shook her head and again sipped her tea. "Not always the case, Captain, as we Issians know that around you lies a very special force—a simple navy captain perhaps, but one that we know makes the right decisions, the right choices, the right actions time and time again. You know—especially from your connection to us Issians via your friendship with your own Adept officer, Bram— that we can often see what is coming. Not so much like a direct doorway that is open and we're looking through—rather like a wall of doorways all with different results, but some are brighter and closer to our brains. It's those ones that often want to happen, and it's those ones we try to send our champions toward. Champions like you, Captain. Will you be our champion yet again?" she asked, and this time he knew she too spoke the truth.

He looked out at the farm that lay fallow and thought for a moment *about what that might mean.*

He wondered what giving assent to this question— mandate really—might mean.

He guessed that once again, his life was about to change, and he looked at the small woman opposite him.

"Two years, Captain. I will be the Master Adept for only two more years, yet I want to help guide Eons back to a full robust future—and to do that, we need you to help. Will you help, Captain?"

He frowned a bit and said, "Two years only?"

She nodded. "Yes, Captain, having the abilities that we do—at least at a Master's level, means that we know of our own demise. Mine is two years away, which means that my work over the past few decades to find and train my replacement is about done. But I also have other tasks to complete too—and one of them involves yourself and the Barony—the Lady St. August, in fact. You will wed her in the next year—and yes, I accept your invitation to perform the ceremony for you two," she said in a matter-of-fact tone.

He was floored by that and looked at her, his mouth wide open. "But ... but, Master—we were—we are—in love, yes, but we can't be married until we work out some issues between us, Ma'am," he said, and he realized if the Master could see this, then it must be true.

She nodded. "Not important for now. Before that ceremony, we must ask you for help in something else. Something is pending that will affect our

Issian way of life—my successor, in fact. We need you to be forewarned and so be forearmed— literally, I'm afraid, this time, Captain, so that you will be successful for us. And for you and the lady as well," she said.

He thought for a second she'd just added that last bit, but he couldn't tell, of course.

"Ma'am, what is it you need done—I'd best know about it in its entirety before I can truly help. Oh, and I want Bram here too, Ma'am, if that's allowed?"

She nodded and waved at a far aide who had been standing alone way down the room's length, and from a door down there, Lieutenant Bram Sander entered the room and walked up with a grin to shake his hand first.

"Oops, sorry, Captain," he said as he snapped to attention and saluted.

Tanner grinned, saluted back, and patted the sofa beside him.

"Ma'am, if only you could provide the lady in such fashion, with all our issues worked out too— that'd truly be a great day," he said ruefully.

She nodded and turned a palm upward toward him. "Some things for we Issians are easier than others—but I can tell you that before you leave Eons and this duty mission, you will be back spending nights on the *BN Sterling*," she said, and

Tanner almost blushed.

"So to our circumstances now and the back story behind them," she said, launching a long tale about the uppermost echelon of the Issian sect and its Inner Circle that governed Eons too. It took her almost an hour to explain what she had to teach Tanner, and Bram learned much at the same time.

When she got to the current situation, and the issue of the Twins Cooperative and Kendal, the part about Mariam also came to light. She wasn't proud of that and tried to downplay the Issian culpability in the issue, but Tanner couldn't not ask about it, digging deeper into their guilt. The fact that the Issians played god with this kind of method to strengthen their Inner Circle members was one thing—but that they had messed it up was beyond his ken.

"Ma'am, wait. If the Inner Circle has nine members and all of you are the living twin except for one, then I have to ask, what happened with this Mariam. Did you not explain that the one twin is— what did you call it—culled from the two? That even you had a twin that was stillborn? So Mariam ... what happened there?" he asked, *and he was not happy with what he'd just learned.*

She nodded and sipped her tea one more time. "It was an oversight that the twin was not stillborn is all I can say, as it happened early in our process of the weaning of the twins, and no one really knows how that happened. It cannot happen anymore, as our medical group and our Inner Circle team handle this with ease—not that the taking of a life is anything but sadness. Yet, it does protect our Issian way of life," she said, and her tone, Tanner thought, was still a bit self-serving.

"So I take it then that this Kendal is the issue? But she's located up on the moon—and the event is in, what, three weeks at the academy—what's the problem then that you will need help with?"

"Mostly, we want you to learn anything extra that you can—I believe you call it recon, correct?"

He nodded.

"Then we'd just ask for that—we want you at the event, and we want you as knowledgeable as possible—can we ask for that help?" she said as she looked at him.

He again nodded and smiled. "I don't know much yet, Master—but I will learn as much as I can. You, Bram—anything to add?" he asked quietly.

Bram shook his head and said, "Not a thing, Sir. That is what is needed …"

Tanner got up and went to the window to once again look out at the farm far below.

Above it, yet below where he stood, a hawk, a square-winged bird of prey floated above the deserted paddock and corrals, looking for food. It knew certainly how to hover, twist and float so that it had maximum time to look down and study the ground cover for its next meal. As Tanner watched, the bird slowly made its way farther and farther away, gliding and floating away...

#####

The big deal, Kendal thought, *about this kind of event was that it got almost no notice from the press— vids, papers, and publishers saw the normal meetings here at the Aporia City Council as boring. Who came, who said what, what budget funds were allotted for this or that—not a single thing was ever new or newsworthy,* she thought, *hence the usual lack of media folks.*

"And this time is the same," she said to herself, as she looked up at the top rows in the press gallery and noted that she and her aides had been able to get all of two of them there in the room to cover the new budget decisions on the MedWard construction. The single vid network camera was pointing at her delegation right now, and since she hadn't as yet been asked for an interview, she fumed.

The real message, she knew, *was to listen to her upcoming speech.*

She knew—well, she at least had heard—that the MedWards were now going to be newly enlarged, and that would mean that the city would have to earmark funds for just that construction. They would be discussing today what amounts would be put aside for this. And not a bit of talk or discussion as to what those funds were doing—propagating the whole issue of what the MedWards did and why that was important to Aporia and Eons too.

She settled even farther down in her seat and read the quick messages that came in from her aides in front of city hall.

Two were out front with more than three dozen twins, all bearing signs and holding up placards that read "No Money for Terrorists!!!"

They were stopping everyone they could, handing out flyers that pointed out the facts that the MedWard doctors were dupes of the Issian Inner Circle. These doctors were a part of a larger conspiracy to help keep the Inner Circle in charge of the future of the Issians and the Adepts too. The MedWards, if enlarged, would do even more harm to the Issian way of life.

Besides the protesters, of course, were the Provost guards who were in charge of security here at city hall—and there was a larger contingent now doing picket duty along the walkways into the building. Anyone could still enter, as they kept the protesters apart from them, and that too was causing a scene she could see on her tablet.

"Change over to the local network," an aide in the row ahead of her said, and as she did so, she noted that one of the Provost guards on the vid feed was boxed in by six protesters—all twins, all female, and all pushing him backward against the flower bed behind him. While there was no real assault, he stepped back right onto the flowers to get some distance between him and them, and the vid feed showed the damage to the flowers in living color.

"Nice," Kendal said, and as she looked down at the council floor, she saw that the Agenda posted on the far screen now showed that the meeting had moved to her area of interest, and she turned off her tablet to listen carefully.

Someone from the riding where the MedWards were located, Riding Five, she thought, was rising to speak and said, in what she'd call a typical politico speech, that the MedWards construction was a needed item for them to simply rubber-stamp today. The new enlargement of the facilities would be looked upon favorably by all of Aporia, and he supported this fully. The fact that Kendal knew, as did most of the people here in the council chambers, that this politician would gain more—much more riding revenues too. This was a simple case of pork, and she almost snorted right out loud but stifled it quickly.

More rose from other ridings. All were in favor of

the expansion of the MedWards and all said so.

The council clerk let each of the various council representatives speak and then looked over to the mayor and said, "Mister Mayor, our listed speakers on council is complete. We now move to allow the public list of authorized speakers. Calling speaker number one on the verified list, one Nelson Corbett of Riding Five? Please come forward ..." she said.

The room quieted as an older gentleman got up from the very front row of the public seating and went down to the microphone placed at one end of the big horseshoe-shaped council table. He tapped the microphone twice and then began to talk in a very soft voice, and someone on the council interrupted him almost immediately and asked if he could please speak up louder.

He nodded and then went on at the same volume to list his own grievances about the new MedWard construction—most of which made actual real sense, Kendal thought. It would be very, very intensive construction with high noise levels within the Dome itself. The lack of real foresight in this regard, the man said, meant there was going to be a ton of extras to fix mistakes and errors, and the construction would last far too long. He finished his five allotted minutes with a plea that such construction should not be allowed and asked the council to not fund the project at all.

The council clerk nodded, made some notes on her tablet, and then said, "Speaker number two is Kendal Steyn, of Riding One," and Kendal rose to take her own place at the microphone. She didn't take any notes or her tablet at all; instead, she grasped the microphone stand with both hands. and in a very strident and loud voice she spoke.

"You must not fund this MedWards construction —as it would be funding terrorists."

Gasps echoed from some in the room. Not a single council member, however, said or did anything but stare at her.

"You all know me—Kendal Steyn—and I run the Twins Cooperative group storefront grassroots organization here in Aporia. We know what you all do not know that the Issian Inner Circle controls the MedWards and their medical staff. And that the Inner Circle is killing twins—via the doctors at the MedWards too. We know that. You all know that. What we then want to know is—why would you fund this kind of Issian terrorism?" she said, and she stopped and looked at each and every single one of the council members still staring at her.

"A part of my five minutes, we were told, would allow us to play a short vid—please direct your attention to the screen," she said, as it suddenly darkened and then everyone was looking inside the MedWard room of a patient, who was tied down—

restrained the doctors called it—to her bed.

She was facing the other way from the camera, but her tangled hair was knotted and very unkempt.

Her bare skinny legs jutted out from below the gown, her leg hair was long, and her toenails were long, curled under the toes, and a dull yellow.

She was tossing one arm trying to get it loose, but the tie-downs were solid, and she failed again and again.

As her head thrashed, the camera could see she had an open sore on the close temple. Pus was caked on the sore and dried up blood surrounded it.

Then she turned her head over to face the camera.

And it was Kendal's face.

Ragged and ravaged and ugly, but it was Kendal's face, now frozen on screen at the end of the video.

The gasp from the council chamber room was loud and very audible.

"That is my twin—Mariam. Our mother was Master Colleen, one of the Inner Council more than forty years ago. She was pregnant and the Inner Council tried to take her embryo and make twins. They succeeded and yes, I'm the one who got her sister's share of all things that make one human.

But instead of being stillborn, Mariam was born as you see her now. There but not there. Alive but not alive, and a prisoner in the MedWard for decades now," she said flatly.

"This is why you must not fund this terrorist project," she said flatly and was silent.

As the single media person continued to film, not a word was said in the council chambers. Two still photographers who'd taken closer seats were already in the way, butting past the few Provost guards who were trying to keep things neat and orderly, but that video of Mariam still was frozen on the screen. The photographers were shooting the screen and Mariam and then shooting her too, to compare, she thought.

The mayor banged his gavel over and over, and more than five of the city councilors had risen to be recognized so that they could speak to this troublesome news to no avail. The clerk herself had heard something that obviously bothered her too, as she fled her desk, it seemed, but then she opened up a side wall door, and more Provost guards entered and took up stations around the council chambers.

Kendal just stood at the microphone.

She had made the choice just days ago to publicize her sister's imprisonment, to let the RIM know of what the Inner Circle was up to in order to keep its power.

She knew that *not a single question would be asked of her.*

She knew that *the frozen face of her twin, Mariam, on screen still looking down at the chamber itself, would speak for her.*

She knew that *this would be all over the airwaves, press, newspapers, and even perhaps Gallipedia too.*

She'd already uploaded the video of her sister's bondage to the Twins Cooperative page there, and she knew that *later today the analytics would show her what kind of a response her tactics here today would bear...*

#####

Bram walked with Tanner to the flyer at the Dessau landing port and smiled as they got to his little blue flyer. They were in the middle of discussing the meeting they'd just had with the Master Adept when Tanner's PDA rang on his wrist.

He nodded to Bram and then said, "Play message" to the AI on his PDA, and above the unit, a small hologram appeared all in monochromatic teal blue. The face was the face of the Lady St. August, and Bram, seeing that, walked away a few yards to play with his own PDA to give Tanner some privacy.

"Tanner—it's me. I'd very much like to see you—

could you come to the *Sterling* tonight for dinner?
So we can talk?" she asked politely. No mention of
anything else—no sorry and no forgive me for
putting you on such a shitty duty mission. Nothing
but dinner, the invitation said.

He nodded and said, "PDA, acknowledge
receipt of message. Send back a yes, I'll come to
dinner at nineteen hundred hours. See you then.
Normal signature," he finished off, and his RSVP
done, he said, "PDA off," and the teal blue
hologram disappeared.

Bram came over and smiled. "Appears that as the
Master Adept said, you two will be back together—
and a wedding in a year! Wow ... will that be a
party!" he said with a slap on his captain's
shoulder.

Tanner half-smiled. He didn't react with more
interest, as he knew that what an Issian saw—even
the Master herself saw—sometimes did not happen.

*He knew that this might happen ... but then also that
an asteroid could come down and send Eons back into
the stone age too.*

*At least that's what he told himself. But there was no
denying Bram was a happy camper.*

He sighed once more and sat in the flyer as Bram
climbed in beside him.

Today, over at Tower Number Three, he was
going to sit in on the Gallipedia installations at the

student library, and he was looking forward to it as he did have a soft spot in his brain for the galaxy-sized resource that Gallipedia was.

Moments later as they lifted off and he spun the flyer to the west, he made one small loop around the *Sterling* as she sat on landing pad number fifty-three. The Barony frigate was, as always, perfectly turned out. Shiny. Her Barony logo of the twin blue and red crowns shone so much it looked like it had been freshly re-done. Down on the tarmac, some chandlers were in-loading something in cases, and he noted the EliteGuards had a couple of squads out doing calisthenics, and even from up here, he could see the sweat and effort these Royal guards were putting out.

As he spun farther to the west, he kicked down on the throttle, and the flyer accelerated up and away. In less than fifteen more minutes, remembering that this was Bram's first trip to the new academy, he dropped down and made loops of all four towers. He even flew the canyon too for a mile or so. As he came up by the big yellow stain of some kind of ore in the canyon wall, Tower Number Three appeared, and he gunned the flyer up and over the canyon rim as he completed the loop and dropped her down agilely onto the tarmac of the tower landing pads.

As they strode by the Provost guard at the

landing tarmac gate, he nodded to Tanner but called over Bram to officially login for the first time. He grinned at Tanner.

"So ... do just we Issians get this kind of treatment, or do all of us get same?" he wondered, as they walked away from the gate toward the now closed massive double doors that led into the tower ahead.

"All of us—guess it's how they know who belongs and who doesn't," Tanner said back, and as they reached the walkway in front of the doors and stepped on the huge plate of blue granite that had just been laid down, the doors swung open.

"Nice touch," Bram said, and they walked into the tower.

In its finals stages of finishing off all the construction shortfalls and extras, there were still contractors, student cadets, and construction supervisors all over the lobby. Some were discussing items that only meant something to themselves, while others were pointing at small pieces of green tape that final inspectors had placed where there was a problem.

Tanner and Bram got in a queue to go up to the library floor in the tower. Floor four was the main library floor, and in a few more minutes, they were there.

As they entered, Tanner was glad to see there

must have been a division of cadets already ensconced in row after row, stack after stack, placing books and updating their tablets. Yes, electronic books also existed, but like most people who did research, you couldn't somehow define the feel of a book, yet the information you got from same by far outweighed what a tablet could say. *Somehow*, Tanner thought, *the heft of a real book meant more.*

At the side on the left, they were greeted by a library staff member, and she smiled at them and ushered them down a long corridor, one side stacked with books on dollies ready for their placement. At the large doors at the end of the corridor, she opened the door, and Tanner and Bram found themselves in a meeting room and went to sit off to one side. They were there to watch and learn and not to contribute—but Tanner knew that he might have to speak up should the need arise.

In another twenty minutes, all the meeting attendees must have arrived as there were now ten of them sitting at the table. *Three were from Faraway,* Tanner noted, *their tails all docile, so no problems there yet. One more was from Skogg, his purple skin really quite dark, almost plum colored, which was an unusual shade for this kind of alien. He was surprised to see an Enkian there too with a black and lavender crest of feathers on his head.*

"Resources, yes?" Bram whispered, which got a nod from Tanner—a crest of black and lavender meant this Enkian was from the Resources Muse— the ones that ran the planet, in fact. He'd had enough of how the different muses engaged with each other already. And yet Enki had been a newly annexed planet, in the Caliphate realm, and yet here they were at a meeting about the academy library.

"Odd, perhaps, but interesting," Tanner thought to Bram, and he nodded, as he'd gotten that thought.

The head of the meeting was a library staff member—one that neither Tanner nor Bram knew —and she called the meeting to order and went around the table introducing everyone.

The human from inwards, who was here representing the Gallipedia interests, was interesting for sure.

"A woman, about fifty or so in years if one can tell anymore," Tanner said to himself.

She was dressed in what might have been very much in style inward in the galaxy, yet here on the RIM, such an outfit of closely fitted small scales of some kind of shiny metal made her look like an old medieval soldier of some type. Her hair looked like it had been doused with some kind of metal sparkles, and they were of all colors, and he assumed that they too were in style. Somewhere. The fact that the only human skin one could see was on the woman's face and hands really didn't matter, he supposed.

The first one to talk on the Agenda was the Gallipedia representative, so while she didn't rise, she did speak loudly, pointedly, and to each and every person at the table.

"My job here today is simple; I have been instructed to acknowledge that the RIM Confederacy has fulfilled all of the necessary applications, paid it's fees, and has therefore been granted CONDITIONAL status as a Gallipedia node in the galaxy-wide network," she said, as her gaze swung from attendee to attendee.

CONDITIONAL? Tanner thought. That's how it worked, he supposed, but he was not alone on that point.

"CONDITIONAL?" the attendee from Skogg said in a voice that was questioning yet somehow sounded ominous.

She nodded. "Yes, CONDITIONAL means that if all goes well in the first year—we will then grant the FULL membership, and the academy will be a node for one and all to see and use." She said it so matter-of-factly that everyone in the room seemed to accept that.

Except the alien from Skogg, previously introduced as one of the members of the Board of Directors for the Academy, didn't accept that.

"Pardon me for asking, but is this the normal way that a university like the RIM Confederacy Naval Academy is granted Gallipedia membership? A CONDITIONAL entry level position—when the academy, at least over at its original location, has already been a full member for over, what, hundreds of years already?" he drilled down on that point once more.

He seemed to have caught the Gallipedia woman out in the open as she actually squirmed in her seat. She looked down at her papers in the file in front of her and riffled through some of same, Tanner thought to buy time.

Eventually, she had to look up at the Skoggian and then the whole table.

She looked a bit perturbed but finally did answer.

"Not normally, no. But we—Gallipedia—have received some ... uh ... some information from various sources that the academy, while on Eons and therefore under control of the Issians here, is having some issues with what I'll refer to as internal conflicts. Something, we were told has yet to come to fruition. So, like all organizations run for the good of its members—the whole galaxy—we have taken the simple precaution of granting

CONDITIONAL membership to the new academy. I'm sure that whatever it is that is in flux will work itself out in the next year …" she said, her voice trailing off.

No one spoke.

Not a word.

Someone, Tanner thought, *had gone to Gallipedia and had told stories out of school—on what he had no idea.*

But this was interesting for sure, and he wondered who that had been … who had tried to subvert the full membership renewals…

At nineteen hundred hours, Tanner presented himself to the EliteGuard who stood on watch at the boarding ramp of the *Sterling*—the Lady St. August's personal frigate. He nodded to the guard and then waited while he checked his tablet. The guard said, "Good to go aboard, Sir. Deck Nineteen is your destination, Sir," and he grinned at the guard and went up the ramp.

Like all frigates, the *Sterling* was a vertically stacked craft. Down the long axis of the ship, for its three hundred feet, lay the lifts and shafts that carried the supporting infrastructure of the ship. Each of the ship's twenty decks was stacked one above each other, and as he was going up to nineteen, he already knew that he was expected to go to the lady's private quarters.

He smiled. *Been there before. And again tonight,* which got a wider smile as he thought of what that might mean.

And then he frowned as he entered the lift doors and said, "Nineteen" to the elevator AI, and the motion of going up began.

He had walked away from the lady due to issues that he had with a marriage to her.

That was true. But if she had been noodling around those issues and had come up with a way to defeat them, then maybe that's why she wanted to see him. *Maybe yes. Maybe no.*

He knew one thing though for sure—that only by working out the issues of a commoner marrying a Royal could their union work.

The door ahead of him opened up by sliding into the lift wall, and he took a step out into the deck corridor.

And he stopped cold.

Why am I doing this, he suddenly wondered as he stopped to think on that for a few minutes.

He knew that seldom—so seldom that he'd never been a part of such an occurrence—did a Royal change their mind.

It might mean that Helena was not going to consider his issues with their marriage.

Which might mean that she was using herself as a lure to try to get him to change his mind—and he couldn't help but grin as that was a threat that he understood well. She was the prettiest—the most beautiful—woman he had ever made love to …

From around the curved walls in front of him came a voice, her voice …

"Tanner … are you dawdling, honey?"

The voice was like liquid love to him, as she slowly came around the corridor from his left.

He took a step out from the lift and turned to face her squarely.

She was in a color he'd never seen before— something between amber and orange and gold. Dressed in a set of what he'd call leggings and a matching top, she wore very high heels, and her hair was stacked up with the same color somehow on sparkles that glinted at him in the deck lights. He nodded and couldn't say a word, as she came right up to him, slid into his arms that now embraced her, and kissed him. Kissed him again. And then one more time.

Lost. I'm lost, he thought, as he continued to hug her tightly, and she twisted in his grasp to walk with him, arm in arm, down the corridor. Only a few feet, but in those feet he realized that the Master Adept would be correct. There would be a wedding and she'd officiate at same, if he could talk

Helena into it.

And he smiled down at her as they crossed the threshold of her quarters and she spoke again.

"AI, secure these quarters. No entry by anyone—Barony code Q-Twelve—confirm ..."

"Confirmed, Ma'am" the AI voiced her receipt that it had complied and that all was as she demanded.

"AI, turn off your monitoring of these quarters 'til say eight hundred hours tomorrow. Barony code Q-Twenty-two—confirm ..."

"Confirmed, Ma'am. Shutting down all AI activity in these quarters 'til eight hundred hours tomorrow."

While Tanner couldn't discern it, he was sure that the AI wasn't happy with being off and not monitoring the heir to the Barony. But then he remembered that one of his comments the last time he'd been with Helena in this very room had been that he'd always felt that with AI being on and monitoring him, he wasn't trusted by Helena either. He hadn't said that exactly, but still he felt that way.

That one's been handled, he thought.

Wonder what else she's come up with?

He sat where she said to sit, over in the kitchen area that she had been cooking up a storm in, and he smiled at her when she handed him the corkscrew.

"You know how to use that, I believe", she said, as she continued to hold it, and he had to wrestle it from her fingers.

"Yes, Ma'am, I surely do. Might I ask what vintage we'd like to begin with this evening?" he said, as he glanced over at the compact wine rack built into the wall of this big kitchen island.

She danced around the other side and lifted the lid on a large red cast iron oven skillet that sat on top.

"Tonight, we're having a big Jambalaya—one whose recipe came from a friend I have over on Turljis—one of our Barony realm worlds, Captain. It's chock full of seafood and sausage, and the rice is to die for—so let's have a wonderfully buttery Quaran Chard, shall we?" She went back to her stove-top, and while Tanner fought the cork out of the bottle, she chopped a couple of herbs up and tossed them into the skillet. She also stirred what he thought must be the rice, and moments later after a quick taste, she nodded and strained it in the sink. Pressing out the last of the boiling water, she then lifted the lid to the jambalaya and deposited all of that rice right on top. A few quick stirs later, the top went back on the meal as she turned off the burner.

"Twenty minutes to let the mix all meld 'til dinner's ready," she announced as she came around to sit on an island stool beside him.

She picked up her glass, and smiling at him, she took a small sip and swirled the wine around in her mouth. Her blue eyes opened up, and she almost lost the snippet of wine she was tasting as she smiled and then swallowed it.

"Gosh, I love Chardonnays," she said and then took a much bigger taste as she swirled the wine in the glass. The legs of the vintage even Tanner could see from feet away were big—and he took a gulp of his own.

She looked at him then, and putting down the glass, she took both of his hands in her own.

"Tanner—I want to be totally honest with you. I want there to be no areas of our relationship that we hide from each other. I want to be in love with you —I am in love with you. And I don't want that to stop," she said, and as he was about to speak up, she held up her hand to stop him.

She slid around on her seat for a moment and then looked back at him, those blue eyes lit with what he'd always remember as love for him.

"I am the heir to the Barony. I can never ever give that up—it's what I was born and raised to be. As you may know, my mother died at my birth, and until my father, the Baron, remarried, I've never had a mother figure. Not that the current Baroness is such a person—what I mean is that it's now going to be up to me to bear the next heir. And I want that child to be our child, Tanner. I want to marry you, and I will do whatever it takes to accomplish that for myself and the Barony too," she said, and her voice was shaky and tremulous.

She looked at him plainly. "Anything—whatever it takes …"

He looked at her, and a smile broke out and he nodded.

That's all that he did. He nodded and she launched herself off her stool and into his arms.

It was all he could do to not tip over backward, but he somehow was able to stand, and lifting her, he carried her out of the kitchen area to her bed in the next room.

Hours later, when the jambalaya was in a big deep-sided dish lying between them on the bed and they were both eating it up with big smiles, he spoke.

"Helena. Dunno why I said what I said months ago—but I think we have a chance to be happy. The Master Adept does so too, I'd add, and she's already said that we marry in the next year—and she added that she'd love to perform the ceremony for us," he offered, and Helena tilted her head to think on that for a moment.

"A year, eh? Okay, time's short, as there is so, so, so much to plan and do. Will happen on Neres, of course, in the palace. We'll have no more though than, say, five thousand guests—I so hate big weddings," she added, and while Tanner tried to restrain himself, his eyebrows arched up at that.

She nodded to him and waved her fork around to emphasize her point. "You've perhaps never been to a head of state wedding before—but it's a bloody big deal. We'll have each of the RIM Confederacy realm's heads—or their designates—there, our own planetary representatives and entourages and families ... it's a big deal, Tanner. You'll see ... it takes hours for us to just meet and greet the heads of state only. Palace will be good for that—oh, guess I have to tell the Baroness today too."

She stabbed a shrimp, then used her fingers to pile on some of that rice, and popped the big forkful into her mouth.

As she chewed that up, he thought *he'd never been happier.* He was sitting with the most beautiful woman in the RIM and working out the details of the wedding as they munched on a late dinner. *Wouldn't have been so late if they hadn't made love the three times, but those memories he had to file away or else the jambalaya would have to wait again.*

"Oh," she said and she pointed her empty fork at him, "you'll need to come up with your best man and your groomsmen too. Bram?" she asked, and he nodded.

No one else really—but then he thought about Admiral McQueen, and he knew he had to have a place for him too. Alver, Kondo, Craig from the Marwick, and even Ahanu from Throth came to mind, and he smiled as he took a sautéed scallop and added it to the half mouthful he already had partially been chewing on.

"Not trying to upset you," he started with, which got Helena to pull back her head and stare at him, "but do you think that the Issians had anything to do with this ..." he said as he waved his own fork at her and him.

She leaned back, grabbed a half glass of Chardonnay, and took a quick gulp before passing it to him.

And she nodded.

"I think that most of the RIM is under their ... their ... spell. Not control, but somehow that the Master and her Inner Circle do their best at the arranging of items for their benefit. Sometimes big —sometimes small. But yes, I did get the idea to send you here to Eons from my Gillian—my own Adept," she said, as she searched in the big pot for more shrimps.

He looked at her and nodded back. Agreed. The Issians were like puppet masters to a degree—not always right and unable to sometimes prevent some happenings especially when they came from outside the RIM.

"Once this damn academy launch is over, you'll be back on the *Atlas*—that suits, yes?" she asked, as she moved items around in the pot.

He nodded and watched the woman whom he loved search for a shrimp.

Finding one, she chortled and again tucked some rice on top and jammed it into her mouth.

He put his fork down and leaned over to kiss her, and she had to stop chewing as they brushed lips.

She pulled back, chomped the mouthful, swallowed it, tossed the fork over her shoulder, and leaned ahead into him for a real kiss.

Bye-bye, jambalaya, he thought...

CHAPTER EIGHT

One of the best classes he'd ever been in, in his own naval academy days, was the one simply titled RECON.

He remembered the professor who'd taught that class and his devotion to details and getting as much information as you could find, beg, borrow, steal, learn, study—the term didn't matter. What did matter was that before any starship captain made a choice that his crew depended upon for their very lives—was that the captain had all the information that there was on that issue.

All the information. No matter what the cost to acquire same, he'd been taught, which was why he now sat on a public shuttle cruiser, in a window seat in civvies, looking out the window. Checking in had been a snap. He showed his hard copy ticket or a screen on his tablet, and it was scanned and beeped, and he walked aboard the shuttle.

From Eons up to its moon, Tavira, was only about a quarter of a million miles. The moon itself was of average size, which he'd learned from the vid that ran on the seat back in front of him, and only about two thousand miles in diameter. Gravity was about a sixth or so of Eons, which meant he would be able to jump a hundred feet or so—not that he'd ever be outside the dome where the AI controlled all including the gravity. No difference, the vid said, between walking on a street in Dessau or up on Aporia either.

He smiled at the little girl who was on the other side of the empty seat beside him, and she blushed and looked away.

Folks who wanted to see Aporia and the moon all took one of these quick shuttles up to the landing port there, and this one was like all the others. There was seating for about forty people and vid screens in the back of all the seats. A couple of flight attendants walked and chatted with passengers for the forty-minute flight. While he couldn't see the bridge, he knew, as he'd checked on Gallipedia, that there were two pilots up there and an engineer who looked after the docking and such at both ends of the trip.

Three chimes went off, and almost everyone

jockeyed for a position to see out the windows.

The video had said that when the shuttle was going to go through the ring that hung above Eons, the chimes would sound, and he too looked out the porthole window beside him.

"Just a tourist looking out the window," he said to himself.

As the pilot had taken the shuttle to the inside edge of the ring, he could see that the man had aimed at slowly moving through the ring where there was a small break a few miles wide in the ice pellets. Made from water with a trace of metals, the ring was only a few hundred miles wide and was less than a mile in thickness. Each of those ice pellets, the vid had stated, was in sync with all the pellets around it. It was a ballet of shiny icy shards, pellets, and pieces from less than an inch across to less than twenty yards wide. Billions of them, it had been determined, lay in this ring and had done that for billions of years. Some had theorized that because of the existence of the ring, Eons had floated the ten or so lights outside of the galaxy. Others thought that the planet had moved there on its own and some other cataclysm had created those ice shards, which when they left the galaxy had been captured by the Eons gravity well.

Didn't matter to me, Tanner thought, as he and rest of the shuttle passengers oohed and ahhed as their ship went slowly through the glistening ice ring.

"*Nifty,*" he said to himself and noted that once through, the pilot yawed to starboard and the ring dropped away quickly. The next stop was Tavira at the Aporia landing port. It took only about twenty more minutes, and Tanner couldn't even feel the inertial dampeners, but the shuttle drifted first to port, then past the force field, and into the secure landing port in Aporia.

Most of the other passengers were up, and the aisle was full of them clutching their carry-on bags, and he noted that even the little girl who he'd grinned at earlier carried what looked like a stuffed animal—a Jael, if he wasn't mistaken. He shook his head at that choice ... how someone who made toys for children would use a beast of an animal and make it look happy and pink was beyond him. He'd faced that creature years before with the duke on a private hunting party and had spent time afterward in a robo-doc recuperating.

Still shaking his head, he rose, and with no carry-on bag, he waited for the lineup to exit in front of him before he even got into the aisle. He walked, following along, through the gate connector to the Aporia Station and then across the big marble floor of the arrivals lobby.

"*Recon,*" he said to himself, as he went out the front doors to the lineups of robo-cabs and dome tour buses and thought about that for a second or two. He needed to learn as much as he could in the two hours before the shuttle trip back, so he got in the short lineup for one of the dome tours and paid his entry fee. It was one of those taller two-floor buses, and he went up to the top deck to get a seat and settle in. After only a few more minutes of loading other passengers, the bus started up, and it appeared the driver doubled as the person doing the explaining of what they saw.

Pulling out of the landing port area, the bus was slowed down by the amount of arriving and departing traffic, but in ten minutes, it was slipping along the roadway leading ahead to the city of Aporia and its thirty thousand inhabitants. As the bus got closer, traffic did thicken a bit, Tanner noted, but the bus driver was pretty good and avoided a real slowdown ahead by judicious lane changes.

As the bus turned onto one of the main streets of the city, the driver began his spiel on various facts about the city and its history.

"Aporia, home for almost thirty-two thousand people, has a rich history which goes back three hundred years to its founding. Before that, the site was a simple scientific outpost that grew and grew for almost five hundred years on its own. But back three centuries, the Master Adept felt that a full city should be established here on the Eons moon—and Aporia the city was born," he said.

"*Page two,*" Tanner said to himself and then grinned at the scenery going by.

"Aporia was designed to be twenty ridings of various locations and populations back then. Since, we've adjusted those riding boundaries and have learned too how to modify the various zonings within so that the city as a whole is a success. Right now, we are in Riding Number Nine, and as we approach the city's major downtown shopping area, we'll move over to Riding Number Seven."

As the bus went on, the driver went on too—telling stories about the city and its past. He did, however, take a stop in front of the Aporia City Hall, and he explained about the current roster of riding representatives and the mayor too.

Must have been on the mayor's payroll, Tanner thought, as the driver glowingly painted a picture of a hardworking, passionate man who ran city council to make Aporia great.

Starting up, the driver swung to the left at the next big street intersection, and for a while, all Tanner could see was shops and stores with sidewalk displays of various goods, trinkets, and souvenirs. Guessing that there would be a stop here, he was happy to see that he was right, and he got off with everyone else to look at the items. He did find a great little knick-knack—the Aporia dome and the city lay inside, and if you shook it, the dome was suddenly filled with snowflakes. It made him chuckle and he bought it and tucked it into a coat pocket.

Back on the bus, the driver took off to go to the very edge of the dome and turned on what was called Dome Boulevard, which he explained ran all the way around the inside of the dome for the full five miles across the diameter. On the left of the bus, the dome itself curved down to sit on a large metal framework that was at least a dozen feet tall. On the right of the bus, across the street from the dome side, ran houses all the way down the block as the road curved always to the right.

He spoke at some length about the various safeguards to the dome architecture as well as what would happen if the dome AI detected a breach in the dome. There had never been one, but being prepared was always a good thing the driver said, and Tanner, like others sitting around him back on the top deck, nodded in agreement.

The bus went slowly and the driver suddenly said, "We have a question from a passenger about the numbering of the houses along the street to your right. As she has noted, they all for the past few blocks start with a two—there's Two-dash-four-five-two-nine and then next here is Two-dash-four-five-three-one. As you can tell, the first digit is the riding—we're in Riding Number Two right now. And all of the street addresses are then in numerical order, odds too in this riding."

Good, Tanner thought, *got that too.*

The bus motored along and the driver filled them up with more news about the dome, its perfect record of no dome breaches, and how the AI was the best on the moon—or Eons too, he noted.

Trusting AI was fine—but only, as all navy men knew, if you had a backup plan ready to roll out if the AI went south.

The bus chugged along, turned ahead at the large light salmon-colored buildings, and slowed as they went by.

"This complex—soon to be expanded, we hear—is the Aporia Medical Wards complex. Where any Eons citizen can go for medical aid for anything from a hangnail to a heart transplant. Been there myownself," the driver said, "as I once fell and broke my ankle—they fixed me up. Robo-doc time was at a minimum, and I was home for dinner that day."

As the bus began to speed up a bit to leave the complex behind, the driver said, "We have another question from a passenger, and I really do not have an answer. Seems he was watching the local vid channel a few days back and saw something about

terrorists being in charge of the MedWards—
something I really doubt, Sir. Maybe you should
ask the vid channel for a full explanation … just
some crackpot, I figure …" the driver said as his
voice trailed off.

And that, Tanner thought, *was about how much
notice the world had paid to this Kendal Steyn and her
video of her twin too.*

He knew this was an item that needed more
recon, but if the real world people thought this was
a conspiracy theory only by crackpots, it might just
die on its own.

He continued to look out at the moon dome
scenery as the bus driver turned toward the landing
port—back to Eons soon…

As her mind joined the Inner Circle group's
meld, it hit her as always like a freight train ... one
instant she was alone on her sofa in her quarters,
and the next she was falling down a cavernous
black hole—a shaft that seemed to go on and on
forever, making nausea come on suddenly.

Then below as she fell, she saw light ... a
pinpoint, but still there was light below.

She had always tried to swim toward it, but she
still couldn't feel her arms as she tried to stroke
toward that light, so she knew to relax and watch as

the light below grew from that pinpoint to a tiny spotlight to a brighter and brighter larger ball of light.

And still the light grew until it was all around her as the blackness receded above her head.

Expectedly, she heard whispers ... many, many voices whispering at her in a language she thought she almost knew but could just not make out the meanings. Those whispers grew and then grew more, intertwining, linking, and building on each other until they were whispers no more but now shouts and shrieks and screams and screeches.

And the mind link was complete, and the Master had just joined in to complete the Inner Circle—the leaders of the Issians.

"We welcome you, Master Adept," all of the minds said in unison, and she nodded back to them even though they couldn't see that motion.

"We have only one topic for today," the Master Adept said, *"and that is the growing issue about Kendal and Mariam and how they might affect our future path."* She fussed for a moment with her small broach of the winged planet that she always put on the bodice of her black robes and then smiled at them all.

"I know—I know. Kendal is not really a threat as yet. But you have seen what I have seen—and the fact is that if she does maintain her initiative of showing Mariam on

that video to RIM citizens — and perhaps to the heads of state on their way here now for the academy opening — the problem gets much worse for us. Much worse. We have too many other irons in the fire, as they say, for our path ahead to grow muddy with old issues. Old mistakes. Counsel here is what I need," she finished off and leaned back.

The talk went round and round.

As every single mind in the link was the mind of a twin, they were all very much aware of the problems of one like Kendal and what she could do. Each had lost a twin via the Inner Circle culls, and each was more superior for just that reason. Each was knowledgeable of what it had taken to get to this level, and each was aware of what it might take to stay at this level of being the elite of the Issian race.

One suggested a simple matter of a moon dome leak — a stray meteor that could pierce the dome and plow right into Kendal's home, ending the problem simply. But that was too random, all had agreed, as the path of that asteroid would have to be aimed by a skilled marksman, but none present was such a marksman enough to ensure no collateral deaths.

One suggested a simple traffic accident, but that was nixed because accidents often are just that, so there was no way to ensure that the correct person was killed.

One suggested poison—a simple spritz or a bump on the bus and Kendal would be gone. That one they could do, and that one they liked enough that it was the leading item to rid the Inner Circle of the threat.

More ideas were suggested but it was not until the last inner circle member, Gloria Patel, spoke that they all knew they'd heard good counsel.

"If the issue is that Kendal will try to disrupt the academy opening, then let's just make it impossible for her to get down to Eons. Make sure she can't buy a shuttle ticket or disable the ship if needs be. That to me is more our style than what I've heard so far," she said with her mind quietly.

Swelling talk around that ensued, and moments later the Master Adept thought right out loud.

"And I agree, too, with Gloria. Most fitting attempt that will be the most hands-off approach that I agree is also more of our own way of doing things. Then we shall simply keep Kendal off Eons. No presence means she can't ambush the heads of state at the big event, and that is what this is all about, correct?"

Murmurs of consent from each member went through the mind link, when Gloria broke in one more time.

"In the future—the near future, I would think—we will need to think about what to do with Mariam too. We

should plan what needs to be done and ensure that our plan is both workable—as well as it comes to an end. Else we may face Kendal again and again …"

Again, consent was thought throughout the Inner Circle.

The Master said her goodbyes and asked only Gloria to remain linked to her. The rest of the Inner Circle un-linked and disappeared.

"Good to see that our backup is still in play, Master," Gloria said, and her mind bowed slightly to her Master, who nodded back.

"Yes, he has no idea yet, but if we need him, Captain Scott will aid us—as far as is necessary. This I do know," the Master Adept said and smiled.

The next Master Adept, Gloria nodded and took her leave, and the current Master Adept nodded now to an empty room.

Seems like the best way to proceed, she thought, seems like the best way…the meteor idea would be serviceable for them…

#####

The analytics did not lie.

No way that the number of views of the vid of Mariam had been tampered with, Kendal thought. Only a bit short of two hundred Aporians had logged in to watch the video. Less than two hundred citizens had learned what their Issian Inner Circle was up to. And less than two hundred people cared—but not a single comment had been registered. Two hundred out of more than thirty thousand inhabitants.

Probably scared—as the vid was about the Inner Circle and how they were terrorists—and no one would make a comment, pro or con, as that would show that they'd actually seen the video. Couldn't hide behind anonymity.

She sighed. She looked once more out her window at the garden and noted that a few of the roses were dead now completely, brown stalks and nodes and the white tinge of mold on the dead blossoms. Amazing what happens when you do no upkeep or maintenance, she thought, which brought her back to Mariam, and she bowed her head on her crossed arms and cried.

She sobbed for a bit, the tears streaming down her arms to lie on the smooth old wooden tabletop in the window of her kitchen, and she cried a bit more too. Her cries lessened and a sudden thought came to her.

Aporia and a city hall council meeting were small potatoes.

Small potatoes compared to a big, big planet-wide celebration.

A celebration like the new opening of the brand new naval academy in about two weeks.

An event she'd seen on the local vid news channel, which would attract dozens of heads of state, the whole academy, and yes, the Issian Inner Circle too was scheduled to attend.

She realized it was big enough that there would be serious press coverage and news vid coverage as well as Eon citizens who needed to know what the Inner Circle was up to.

She half-smiled then as she realized that by being up on Tavira and in Aporia—because that's where Mariam was—was thinking too, too small.

She needed to think big, and that half smile turned into a wide grin.

She went back to the island in her kitchen and onto the net. She went to the local Aporia area and looked for services, and yes, there it was. She clicked shuttle services with a forefinger, and moments later up came a table with dates and times for both up and down shuttle flights. It took her a moment to compare that list with the other page open on her tablet with the academy opening event timetable, but it showed her soon enough that the day she wanted was exactly two weeks today. The academy opening at Tower Number Four was at thirteen hundred hours, so she'd need about a day to get ready. She skipped back to the shuttle timetable and there was a series of five shuttle flights all due to go down to Eons the day before.

She picked one in mid-morning, filled in the short form, and clicked the SUBMIT button.

And waited. And waited some more.

And then she was taken to a page that informed her that flight was fully booked.

She tried all the flights that day and all were booked.

She tried the five flights the day before that, and all were booked.

It was not until after trying ten flights that something clicked in her head, and she began to wonder.

She went back to the shuttle timetable and picked a day to fly six months from now, filled in the form, and was informed that flight too was full.

Something is wrong. The form will not take me as a passenger, she thought with a growing suspicion. There was no way that a date six months from now could be full. She went back to the form and filled it out with her grade three teacher's name, and used a fake address, and clicked the SUBMIT button for a flight the day before the academy opening—and it went through to the payment page with no problem.

Keyed off my name, she realized.

But with security the way it was, she would need … she would need … David.

She got up, and taking her tablet, she went to the

rear bedroom, knocked on his door, and got a "Yeah" in response.

Entering, she explained her problem, at least how she had just learned about same, and he tilted his head and said, "Nah, really?"

His fingers were already flying on his keyboard, and a moment later he too was looking at a screen with a message that the flight was full..

He frowned.

He tilted his head back, looking up at nothing but was lost in thought.

Then he smiled and looked back at her.

"I'll get you booked, Auntie, on the same mid-morning flight, not a problem. But I'd like to come along—that okay?" he asked.

She hesitated then realized that yes, if anyone was needed to help her get that Mariam vid on screen at the academy opening event, there would be no one better than David for that, and she nodded back to him.

"I will need you to somehow, um, interrupt the normal vid streaming and to insert our own. I doubt that I can get anywhere near enough to actually speak to guests and the heads of state, so we need to craft a full video of what we want to say. But as this is the academy where you worked before, this should be easy for you—yes?"

He half-shrugged and said, "At one time, sure.

But new folks and new systems often don't grandfather in old personas—sorry. What I mean is, yes, I've got a back door in place—wait."

His hands flew on the keyboard, and she only recognized a couple of screens as they went by—an official academy screen and then some kind of HR screen—and he slapped his hand down on his desk as he whooped right out loud.

"I would guess that they've just ported over the old academy system database and their HR profiles so that my back-door persona I've always had still works. Yes, I can get into the system, and yes," he said as his fingers began to fly once more, "I can—can't—can maybe this way—doesn't work so how about—yes! I can also see and therefore access the queue for what someone there had called the opening event video tours. Should be easy to—wait," he said and leaned back to look up for a moment.

He tilted his head forward and then nodded.

"Remember a week ago or so when the toaster oven wouldn't accept a timed cook for those nachos?"

Kendal nodded and said, "So I just unplugged the whole oven, counted to ten and plugged it back in to reset the timer. Sure ... why?"

"Because that's what someone will think of after a few seconds of our video. They'll just kill the power to the AV displays," he said, and then he held up a finger.

"But I know a way around that one too, so we're …" he said as he looked up at the ceiling taking stock of their plan, "we're good!"

She smiled. *Having a techie in the house was such a great thing if you're planning to revolt,* she thought

"And the tickets too?"

"Great. Will do—and I'll print out hard copies of those tickets for us to use too," he said, as she smiled at him and left his room.

Lotsa planning to do, she thought, and she went back to the kitchen table to once again stare out at the dead roses and think about what she could do to disturb the plans of the Inner Circle.

#####

When Superintendent Chapman knocked on his door, Tanner was more than surprised to see that the man—one of the head construction men on Tower Number Two—looked so frazzled as he got up to open his office door.

"Superintendent, what can I do for you?" he asked with a soft voice.

The man came in, and going to Tanner's desk, he pushed everything aside, laid out a rolled-up set of blueprints, and stabbed a finger down on a huge red circle that appeared on the sheet.

"We have been working on these plans—EKF Number Ten Twenty-four dash B—since last year. Each set has had spares and extras input from various factions here at the academy. We're used to all kinds of modifications and the extras that come. We know how to read plans and build accordingly. Yet today, we got this set—still labeled as EKF Number Ten Twenty-four dash B—but as you can see plainly, it is different than our own masters," he spit out.

Mad? Was he ever, Tanner thought as he looked down at the plainly easy to read plans and couldn't see what any issue was at all.

He nodded and then said calmly, "Could you elaborate please on that, Superintendent? Because I cannot read plans—something we weren't taught at naval academy—any naval academy, I might add." He leaned a hip on the edge of the desk.

Chapman sort of smiled ruefully and shook his head. "Sorry, but here's the skinny. We built the building according to the plans—we got the updates, not a problem. But today, I was served with papers—including this set of plans—that show that throughout each of the floors that hold faculty offices—they're all smaller than what the plans said. On this set. Not on the ones we built to—but on this set," he said as he drew from an inner pocket a sheaf of folded papers.

"And today, in the Tower Number Two construction offices, we were served with these STOP WORK papers from the Eons Superior Court—an action that was filed by the professor's academic union. A union action ... for God's sake," he said, and he tossed the legal docs on top of the spread out plans. "Court date will be in three weeks —so we can't continue with the final list of shortfalls until then. Which means that next week's academy opening will not happen," he spit out and slammed a hand down on the papers on the desk.

A quick perusal of the legal docs showed that yes, the STOP WORK order had in fact been served today, the court date was in three weeks, and it was duly signed by the clerk of the court and the president of the academic union—one Professor Nigel Watkins.

Um ... Tanner thought, there's a name I know.

Just a few months back, he'd been able to help that professor with a textbook problem. And if he was not mistaken, the professor had offered that should he ever have any issues, he'd be pleased to help.

Tanner nodded to the superintendent and smiled, but he made sure it was a small smile.

"Good of you to come to me," he said "and yes, I think I can help here. Know I can help. Please, Superintendent Chapman, disregard this notice from the courts, I'll take care of it, and we have, what, only a week left before the big day."

"Big day, indeed," the man said, as he rolled up the plans and threw an elastic band around them. "With, what, a dozen or two heads of state, it's the academy's chance to look good in their eyes. And," he said with a bit of self-promotion in his voice, "for us, the construction company, to take some bows too!"

Tanner was sure of that—any firm that could build four fifty-plus-story buildings in a year was one to be reckoned with, and he nodded back to Chapman.

"Spot-on, Superintendent, now back to work and ignore this order," he finished off, and as the man left, Tanner went next door to the admiral's office to talk to the admiral's aide.

Moments later, Lieutenant CoSharan was off the Ansible console and looked at him and he smiled. Better to start with a smile, he thought as the lieutenant's tail was up in the air slightly. Not so much that the Faraway alien was upset, but something was bugging him.

He looked at Tanner and cocked his head, which made Tanner think that human body language characteristics seemed to get copied by just about all the RIM alien races, but he shook off the thought of documenting that and nodded instead.

"Lieutenant, our construction superintendent down at Tower Number Two got this," he said as he laid the sheaf of legal papers on the desk. "And I told him to ignore same—we can deal with this—and to not stop work on the last week before the opening. Did I do okay?" he asked.

The lieutenant went through the papers one by one, nodding, and then folded them back up.

"Captain, if we do not get this put into abeyance, in that the local union cannot get such an action as the academy is a RIM Confederacy property, we might be in trouble. But I know a couple of clerks down at Superior Court—I'll make the call. But I also noted that the action was filed by an academy professor, one Nigel Watkins, and all I can say is that this man is the singular cause of much of the delays we've faced up until, I think, a few months back. Been quiet since then though ..." he said, as he made some notes on a tablet, copied the STOP WORK certificate numbers, and then handed them back to Tanner.

"Got it, Lieutenant. And I'll have a word with this Professor Watkins too—will not stir the pot at all, don't worry. But if you can work the court angle, we'll be fine, I'd bet.

The tail on the alien was now lying flat on the floor, poking out of his specially made office chair, Tanner noted.

Good sign.

"Any idea where I can find this prof, Lieutenant?" he asked, which got him a nod as he was told that it'd be relayed to his PDA in a few minutes as soon as the aide could find him.

Smiling at the lieutenant, Tanner went back to his offices and sat and stared at the only artwork that he had put up on a wall, the Enkian painting that had been a fortieth birthday present from the Lady St. August. As he thought that, he realized that he would need to be calling her his fiancée, and that was a thought he found both surprising and yet nice.

The art was of an abstract type that he remembered from his very first tour of the Fine Arts Muse pyramid, done by one of their younglings, as he remembered, and yet the raw, vibrant colors leaped out at him still. He smiled as he looked at the vibrant blues, aquamarines, teals, and azures in the palette and wondered what the names were for the other three bluish types of color.

Professor Watkins was next, and then tonight, he'd need to spend some time thinking about his groomsmen and his best man, who he assumed would be Bram. Helena would be asking him about that for sure later at their late dinner, and the last thing any groom-to-be wants to be is unprepared.

He sighed and then smiled. He'd heard today

that the *Atlas* was bringing in the Baroness to the academy opening event, and he really was looking forward to spending a bit of time with his old crew.

And their captain, too. Kondo must be doing a great job, he thought with a bit of envy.

CHAPTER NINE

As Kendal and David approached the boarding ramp for the shuttle down to Eons, her grip on his arm tightened.

"Not a problem, Aunt Kendal, honestly. Take it easy," he said for the umpteenth time since they'd been at the Aporia port, and he patted her hand to get her to let up on the squeeze.

She did, but only a little, and he smiled nicely at the young woman behind the ticket check-in kiosk, and she smiled back at him too.

"Tickets, please," she said and accepted the two printed hard copies of both. Glancing only for a second at them, she held them up to the scanner, which beeped three times.

Nodding, she handed them back to the twosome and then smiled at the next shuttle passengers as

Kendal and David walked on.

"And exactly how were you able to accomplish that, David?" she asked, the relief in her voice almost palpable.

He talked as they walked down the long ramp to the tarmac and continued out to the shuttle where they took seats right up front.

"Exceptions, Auntie, the exceptions," he said and looked at her as they settled into their seats.

Kendal was busy trying to jam her small carry-on bag below the seat in front of her, and it took her a moment to get back to him.

"What does that mean—exceptions, David?" she asked.

"Online commerce—like buying a ticket for the shuttle—is normally no problems. After a few thousand years, it's been handled. But sometimes there are what we IT techies call exceptions, which means that something odd has come along and is handled by a different set of code algorithms. Following me here?" He tilted his head and Kendal nodded.

"Good. Well, when someone wants to change a ticket's date of departure—that's an exception. So I logged in—well, hacked in might be a better way to put it—to the shuttle site and waited while I watched for someone who did have today's leaving dates and wanted to change them to a date in the future. That allowed me to both issue to them a future date—as well as to not issue a cancellation of today's date. Problems with exceptions, as you can tell, exist if that kind of change does not issue an alarm—and there was none. So today, as I said earlier, we're the Andersons. Mother and cousin, it said, but that works for us too, right?"

Kendal sat still for a moment and then said, "If that's true, then any hacker could issue like a million tickets to anyone else, right?"

"Theoretically, but after being on the IT staff over at the academy—well, the old one, I mean—for all those years, I do know that most systems do a monthly review. The chance to find us before the end of the month is not possible, but in twenty days or so, they will learn that the Andersons went back to Eons twice. That should mess up their numbers a bit, so someone will get the job to build a handler to handle the routine of ticket date changes. But today, we're on our way back to Eons," he said and looked past Kendal to the shuttle window.

All the passengers appeared to be on board, and liftoff was smooth. As the shuttle headed straight up, the force field around the tarmac dropped off, and they were headed back to Eons.

"And our hotel, David? Will we be the Andersons there too?" Kendal asked as she peered down at the moon dome as it fell away and soon only Eons could be seen ahead and to the left a bit.

"We are not, Auntie. For our accommodation, we've got the next four nights at a hostel—the Wool Hostel—booked under two more names. Did not want to use the Anderson ID any further, so this time," he said as he dug out a piece of paper, "you're going to be one Gladys Bielak—a librarian from Juno, on a simple vacation. I'm," he said, looking down, "one Nelson Outridge, a student going to Eons on his trip to Leudi—I guess I want to be a trader, it seems," he said.

She nodded and then as she turned to ask something, he put a hand down on her forearm resting on the armrest between their seats.

"Nothing to worry about—these IDs are fine. You won't' get asked anything when we check-in, and as we're paying in real credits, we show no IDs at all—course, you should look a bit more library-ish, Auntie," he said as he smiled.

She snorted. "Hair in a bun? Cardigan on and sensible shoes?" she asked.

He laughed right out loud, and they quieted down as the shuttle closed on Eons.

"When we get to the hostel, will it have WiFi?" she inquired and got a nod back from David.

"First thing then, I'll need to buy an anonymous PDA chip to plug in to my unit so that I can message back to my aides up on Tavira. Will need to let them know that I'm sick—say with the Madrigal Flu—so I'll need ten days off with no personal contact. I'll tell them you got it and I've been looking after you for a week and now I got it. That should keep the Twins Cooperative up and running fine but not aware of what we're doing. Which then leads me to your own area—the academy net. New academy means new IT—so are you making any headway with getting into their system?"

He looked away for a moment, then shrugged, and looked back at her.

"Not easy, but yes—sort of. I can't hack in like I used to—what I can access is all small stuff, personnel, suppliers, that kind of thing. What I need is, of course, access to the opening event routines—something that so far is still in their inner queue—programmers only and I'm no longer an academy programmer. But once all things gel, that should be opened up to the normal access for all admins and the like—and I still have a set of those IDs to try. So yes, I'm getting there but not yet," he said.

She just looked at him. "I am counting on you, David. Your Aunt Mariam is counting on you, David, and hundreds of twins yet un-conceived are counting on you too," she said quietly.

He looked away again, and they traveled the rest

of the way to Eons in silence.

#####

In Admiral Higgins' inner office, Tanner, the admiral, and his aide, Lieutenant CoSharan, stood looking at the folding tabletop that had been carried in, placed against a wall, and set up with the academy opening event stage layouts.

What someone had done was to copy the seating arrangements according to the latest list of attending heads of state and then put that name on the back of a little block of wood indicating a chair. Then the chairs had been arranged into rows, and the dais with the microphone was positioned up at the front, looking out at the audience that would be seated out on the tower landing tarmac.

Admiral Higgins looked at it and said, "Well, what are the complaints so far?" in a gruff voice.

His lieutenant said, "Sir, yes, Sir, they're up now." He pushed a button on his tablet, and above the table on the wall, a screen now held bullet points listing issues.

"Sir," the lieutenant read, "the first one is that the Takan and Conclusion heads have bitched about being put in row number two and behind the Eran head of state. At twelve feet tall and in the front row —as was requested by him by the way—he'll block out half the row behind him. Rest of that row probably hasn't even looked at the seating, so they're unaware but will squawk big time once they get here."

Tanner looked back at the layouts, and what the lieutenant said was probably true. Takan and Conclusion were right behind the Eran head of state, so they'd not be seen at all, and as neither was on the list to speak, the audience would never know they were even there.

The admiral looked at him and said, "So ..."

Tanner shook his head, as he really had no answer.

The fact that Eran was populated with an alien race that at full adult height stretched up for a dozen feet made holding any kind of event that they would attend a nightmare for event planners...

"Sir, I note that whomever did the chairs for this display neglected to make the Eran chair three times as wide as any other, and that might have had something to do with this. Is there anyway, Lieutenant, for us to shift the Eran head over to the end of that front row? Still in the front row, but then we can shorten the second row behind him so that all can be seen? Would that work?" he asked.

"Gonna have to—next," the admiral said, and his aide clicked a button, and the next item came up on the screen.

"The Tillion head of state has requested that his

row—note the use of the personal pronoun—that his row has no women in it whatsoever. No surprise there, so we can do this now, right?" the lieutenant said. He moved to the table, and placing the Eran head of state at the far right side of the front row, he picked up two chairs from behind it. He moved one to the third row and the other to the third row on the left side. Then he switched the chairs for Tillion from the front row left-hand side to the second shorter row on the right-hand side.

Tanner could see that the remaining seats in that short second row were now held by Novertag, Duos, and Tillion. Not a woman there, so that would work, and the admiral grunted, "Next!"

The list was still long, and it took almost a full hour to get through to the last item.

The admiral's aide read exactly the final listing with what Tanner could tell had no inflections or values added by him.

"The Leudi head of state has requested that he not only not be seated close to the Faraway head of state—but that he be on the whole other side of the stage from him. The Faraway head of state has made the same exact request, too …"

As a Faraway citizen, with that tail that told all, it was easy to see as it was raised up and pointed at the ceiling that the lieutenant would have loved to have said more—but he didn't.

Good man—rather, good alien, Tanner corrected himself and said, "Simple."

He reached over to the stage layout, picked up the Leudi chair, and dropped it directly onto the second row behind the huge Eran head of state.

"Problem solved, yes?" he inquired, and both he and the lieutenant looked at the admiral.

It was no surprise that the Leudies were not in the good graces of most of the RIM Confederacy realms. It had recently come to pass that their huge margins on an antidote for a recent outbreak of a serious influenza had been leaked—as had the fact that buying the antidote made one addicted to same, which raised their revenues considerably.

The admiral smiled. "Good. Then I take it we're done?" he asked, which got smiles all around, and they moved on to the speakers.

That list was much shorter and had been already vetted by both the Master Adept and Admiral Childs.

"Childs will be the MC but also deliver a keynote address right up front," the lieutenant read off his tablet.

"Followed by the Master Adept, then the Baroness or the Lady St. August—we've not heard back as yet. Of course, rumors are that the Baroness was out on their annexed new planet, Ghayth— more than seventy lights ahead, so I've notified the lady that she may be speaking for the Barony. For a reason that escapes me," he said, and he held up his hands to show that he didn't want to know, "we have a short piece by the local professor's union president—one Prof Nigel Watkins. What he might have to say, I've no idea, but he'll be followed by the head of the construction firm, Superintendent Bill Chapman, who will say nice things too—least he's been instructed to do same. Then Admiral Higgins has a short piece to let them know how they can contact us should they find a shortfall in their rooms or the like, and we finish with Admiral McQueen to welcome the cadets and the grand cutting of the big wide ribbon—scissors for every head of state—and the vids will capture it all.

"Oh, tours of all the tours have been already filmed and will appear on the many vid screens including the huge one behind the stage too so that one and all can get a sense of the size of the project and how well we've all done. Expect that few will say so—but I do think we did," the lieutenant finished up.

All there were quiet. Seemed like a full couple of hours, Tanner thought, but then that's what these things were like.

The last time he was a part of an event like this was on Halberd. As that thought crossed his mind, he flashed back to his time on Halberd at the prison and their 100th Anniversary of no escapes event. That had been ambushed by the prison convicts who had been able to turn off the force field protecting the stage that was even more crammed with heads of state. He'd had to draw his Colt and kill the revolt leader and then the convict's sister who had been aiming at the Caliph to kill him. He'd had to kill both of them that day, and the resulting effects on him—

"Captain," the admiral said, shaking Tanner's arm, "Captain—are you okay?"

Tanner shook it off. The PTSD came so seldom that he was unaware his left hand was beating the one, two two ... one, two two anti-PTSD rhythm on the table. He shook his head once more, jammed his left hand into his pants pocket, and smiled at the admiral.

"Sorry, Sir, lost in thought," he said and backed up and away from the table.

The admiral looked at him out of the side of his eye and then nodded.

"Okay, Lieutenant" he said, moving on, "next ... catering, seating, shuttles from the other towers ..."

#####

It had taken most of last week, but with a plan on the go, the actual doing was a lot more stressful, David knew.

He walked to the corner and breathed deeply, hyperventilating his lungs until he sounded like he was almost out of breath. Turning, he trotted down the block behind him about halfway and went in the outer doors of the cleaners and right up to the counter.

A woman stood in front of him, and yet he went right up to the counter and snapped his fingers in the clerk's face.

"Hello … hello?" he said and snapped them again.

The woman who had been in the process of complaining about some kind of poor cleaning job, done on the sweater on the counter, just stared at him open-mouthed.

The clerk held out a hand to stop him from going on, but he had no time for that.

"Ma'am, my boss is outside in the car—and his Eons Power uniforms are late. Late once again. Dunno if they're on that rack or wherever they are, but we have a big—bloody big—account with you. If you can't give me his uniforms, he's going to come in here and tear a strip off the owner— Herbert, right? And I'd say he'd cancel our annual contract with you. Is that important enough to allow me to butt in on the lineup here?" he said, as he looked at the clerk and then the woman who shrugged.

He dug in his pocket, came up with a twenty-credit bill, and placed it on top of the woman's sweater.

"Ma'am, I'd love to pay to get this re-cleaned—re-cleaned properly, mind you," he said, as he stared at the clerk.

The clerk shrugged and said, "Ticket?"

He looked at her. "Ma'am, I have no ticket, but we never get tickets. Your drivers pick up the dirty uniforms and deliver them. Except that my boss—Foreman Rance Peters—did not get his. That means that they're here, somewhere ... go find them!" he pushed, and the clerk, sensing that this was more important than she'd first thought, nodded and disappeared.

David made small talk with the middle-aged woman and agreed wholeheartedly that the worlds had gone to hell in a hand basket—one just could not get good reliable service on almost any type of job.

Three minutes later, the clerk reappeared with four uniforms all hung and clad in transparent plastic wrap.

"Found 'em—seems the wearer got some kind of almost impossible to remove stains down the side of one of the jumpsuits, so we held all three 'til it was ready too ... sorry about that. But they are all clean and nicely pressed." The clerk stated the obvious.

David nodded and grabbed them down off the hanger stand.

"Fine, but don't ever do that again," he added as he spun on a heel and went back out the door to the left. At the first corner, he found the robo-cab button kiosk and called for one. Dessau was far ahead of Aporia and the simple ability to call a cab using a button was a great example of same.

Twenty minutes later, he was in the Wool Hostel, hustling up the stairs to his room on floor three.

It took him almost another hour to find out more about the Eons Power grid at the new academy and tower Number Four, new lines and all. As he did so, he tried on a jumpsuit and found that as he'd surmised from Peter's own page on the Eons Power site, they shared similar sized frames and waist and chest sizes. Foreman. Now he was going to be a foreman …

It fit. It was about one inch too small in the inseam, but that was all he noticed. He smiled when he saw the name badge proclaimed the word foreman. The white jumpsuit would now be filled with a techie—a hacker—instead of a power expert.

On top of that, he put on a hoodie and a pair of loose jeans to hide the uniform. He looked again in the mirror and thought plain-looking young man— nothing to worry about.

He smiled one more time as he checked his time

on his new PDA and noted it was just before lunch.

He wanted to be there near the end of lunch, so he gathered up his other props, placed them in a white shoulder bag, and took the stairs back down. He also made sure to pack carefully the special battery he'd only gotten this morning before the uniform gathering.

At the curb, he grabbed the robo-cab that was idling, and he inquired if it was equipped to take him out to the new academy towers. The robo-cab's AI replied, "Sorry, we can't get there," but he was also told that the cab could take him to the Dessau landing port, where a shuttle flyer could handle the last part of the trip, and he nodded.

A half hour later, he was in the shuttle flyer almost alone as there was only one other couple on board, and they emptied out of the shuttle as soon as it landed.

David stood and quickly dropped off the hoodie and jeans too, and he now looked like an Eons Power guy. He tucked his clothes into the space below the seat in front of him, and then hoisting the heavy bag over his shoulder, he began to walk toward the stage. He had thirty minutes to get back on board.

A Provost guard, gnawing on what looked like a Skoggian plum, nodded to him, pointed, and said, "Your boys are over there ... uh ... Foreman," and then went back to the plum.

The area he had pointed to was a tented enclosure that luckily was sealed off on this side, and as he left the guard, he commented that he'd see them later as he was here to check their work. From inside came the sounds of some kind of music he'd never heard before, and he was glad to leave that behind too as he strode away.

He went down the far right side of the huge swath of seats, all the way to the front, and then around the huge stage, and then to the back. Working at an audio-visual sound station, a couple of sound techs nodded to him but didn't stop. He went by them to the actual back of the large frame that would hoist up the full vid screen for one and all to see the tour videos. "And more," he said to himself.

He looked down at the cables, and three separate power cables came from somewhere and connected to the screen assembly. The three of them climbed up about ten feet to a big power distribution nexus. From that large distribution node, they then went to three specific spots.

One was very easy to identify as it was plugged into a socket that was labeled Power to Frame-IN.

One more was also easy, as it was plugged into what looked like a splitter box, which sent the streaming video to all the various displays all over the grounds. He lost count at thirty-eight, but that didn't matter. This box was positioned on the rear of the big vid screen about halfway up.

The final power cord went to the router that routed various streams to various displays. Why they'd have that, he had no idea, but all three of the power cables were right in front of him. And he could do nothing with them at all.

When his aunt's vid began to play, someone would think of the big red switch and just turn off all video feeds.

Those switches would be somewhere at master power control and another here at Tower Number Four somewhere, and one could just as easily grab these cables and yank them out. He had thought of that, and the videos would all have a crawl at the bottom of the screen letting services know that all power cables were live—to grab one would cause a massive electrical shock—perhaps even a lethal shock.

The switches before the cables had been the issue he'd fought with all along, and he had an answer.

He went back to the group of sound techies and spoke to one he thought looked more in charge.

"Excuse me? I'm a dumb ass foreman sent to check on the team we have here doing the power install. Might I borrow that ladder there," he said as he pointed at a yellow wooden one leaning up close to the screen frame.

The sound tech never even looked and just waved and nodded.

David went and got the ladder. He moved it over so he could have access to the power distribution node and scrambled up it easily. Once there, he took a look, and yes, there was a big red switch built into the node, and that made him smile.

Pulling out the Ni-Cad battery, he turned it on first and placed it exactly where it would work, on the outgoing side of the node, and then he stopped.

Kill power. Plug the three cables into the battery. Plug the battery into all three ports in the distribution node. Then turn back on power.

It had seemed easy as he'd studied and memorized the plan over the past month.

Here goes nothing. He toggled the big red switch, and around him, some things went off—lights and a hum died too. He yanked out the three cables from the distribution node and plugged them into the battery. He plugged the battery into the three outgoing ports on the distribution node and then hit the big red RESTART switch, and in less than a second, all was well.

Power is back on, and we own the last spot that one could perhaps kill the power to for the opening event videos.

Nodding to the sound techie, he said, "Waste of

time, these guys are good," as he replaced the ladder and moved off once again to round the stage, go past the lineup of seats, and then return to the landing field to the shuttle flyer.

As he got just about off the field, someone behind him yelled something. He couldn't understand what the man had said, but he too was dressed in a white Eons Power jumpsuit.

Not good—especially if this guy actually knew Foreman Peters.

As he reached the Provost guard, the man held out a hand and waved behind him.

He interrupted the guard right away. "Yup, I know—he's one of the slackers whose work I just checked. Gotta turn in my report, so if you could just slow him down so that I can make the shuttle," David said as the props of same had just started up.

With a nod and a wink, the guard said, "You've got it, Sir—hustle now!" as he moved up toward the man who had taken to trotting to try to catch David.

Sliding in the open door of the shuttle, he was pleased to once again note that there were only a couple of other passengers, and he took the same seat. With his foot, he dragged out the hoodie and put it on.

So ... he thought, *so far, so good* ...

David rewound the app's time line, and they sat and watched the video yet again—from the top.

Kendal's face appeared first with a serious look on it. Her hair had been brushed back a bit more than her normal style, but that was good, David had argued, as she now looked a bit more like Mariam.

She spoke slowly but clearly, and her tone this time—they'd tried four others—mad, whiny, satirical, and even happy—was matter of fact. That's what they agreed to call it—just a simple listing of the facts.

The first thing that happened was a sound everyone knew—the chiming of an alert. Yes, David had said, it was a tech sound, but everyone there had some tech experience. They'd all know the trilling alert sounds.

She began with an introduction of who she was.

"Good afternoon to the heads of state and guests. My name is Kendal Steyn, and my mother was a member of the Issian Inner Circle in years gone by. And it is about this Inner Circle that I wish to spend just a few minutes talking to you all."

On screen, she stared directly into the camera.

"Our Issian Inner Circle is being run as a group of terrorists!"

Her tone at the end of that claim was up, and she

increased her volume too, figuring this was the crux of her argument.

"They learned more than forty years ago that the best Issians—the ones of us with the most advanced Issian skills of the mind—could be created. Made. And only in one way ..."

She paused there—David said it helped as she'd just told them that something important was coming, and the delay built the delivery via the suspense.

"They create twins in a new mother's womb; they then take from one twin all of the characteristics and abilities that this twin would have been born with and move them over via mind control to the other twin ... the one that will survive. The twin who was stripped of their abilities to build a super-Issian just across the womb will not survive. They are always stillborn. Sadly, of course, the mother never knows that this procedure is carried out up in Aporia in the Issian MedWards."

She paused again and let that sink in for only a few seconds.

"I know this to be a fact because I am a surviving twin. My own twin was to be stillborn ..."

David had used a great transition to go from her face to the MedWards and Mariam's patient room. Again, the same thirty-five seconds played out with Mariam finally turning to face the camera, and all could see—would see—that this was truly Kendal's twin.

She nodded as Mariam's face faded out and was replaced with hers.

"I ask the gathered heads of state to launch an investigation into this Issian terrorist program … the killing of a twin over and over … to make the Issian rulers of Eons that much stronger. This must not be allowed …"

The inflection on the word must was the most recent change—she pushed it and hoped that all the attendees would agree.

She nodded and looked at David.

He nodded back and said, "And we're done, right?"

She thought about that for a full minute.

She'd presented her case with no real claims that she couldn't prove, and the fact that Mariam's face and hers were a match was the clincher.

She nodded back.

"Yup, we're good, David. But now we need a crawl across the bottom with the don't try to turn this off notice. We need to also be able to watch the presentation too—can we just use a media feed? It will be live reported, I think, all over the planet— even off-world too, so we'll get great exposure."

David nodded and they then planned what the crawl should say and how firmly it should let the viewers know that there was danger if they tried to cut power to the screens.

CHAPTER TEN

"It was one of those days," Tanner said to himself, *"that made you feel alive."*

He'd had a great dinner last night on the *Sterling* with the Lady St. August—and an even better night with her too. He'd awoken today, the academy opening event day, and had smiled when he came down the boarding ramp off the *Sterling* and into the bright Eons sunlight.

No clouds—big high-pressure day was what that meant. The sky was so blue, he could see at least three hundred miles, he thought, as he lifted up his flyer and went west toward the canyon and the new academy towers.

Helena had begged off on getting up this early with him and said her only job was to shower and dress later and give the pretty, standard speech about how happy the Barony was with the building of the new academy. She also said she had to just confirm the contents of the speech with the Baroness, who was on Ghayth, and then take a flyer bus over to Tower Number Four. She said all of that, her face buried in one of the huge pillows with the silk pillowcases, and he smiled down at her, patted her on her bare derriere, and left her to sleep some more.

As the flyer came into Tower Number Three, he saw there was a shuttle there already operating, so he knew he could get over to the administration tower, and he set down fairly close.

His job today was small, yet he was armed, the Colt at his side.

It had cost him almost an hour last night of tossing and turning. *But he knew that if anything happened at the event, while there was a full Provost guard company present, as well as all the heads of states' personal bodyguard squads, he wanted to be armed too.*

He felt that way for many reasons, but what had come to the front of his consciousness was the final rationale that he had been surprised before and had been able to rise to the occasion. So he went armed.

The shuttle yawed and dipped, and moments later, he was deposited off to the side of the enormous tarmac with its thousands of chairs, catering stations, and bars.

He grinned. *In years gone by, he'd have found a station very, very close to one of those bars and would have checked on the Scotch often. And even more often too. But those days were gone ...*

He walked down the temporary walkways that had been added to the shuttle bus landing areas, and while it took a few minutes, he eventually was on the tarmac, about halfway down the rows of seats. He turned to his right to slowly walk again up the empty aisle, and again it took minutes with the various other folks on the aisle. Provost guards were getting assignments. Catering staff was loading up coolers, hot food stations, and all their dollies and large display cases. A few more he didn't have any idea as to what they were up to, until he realized they were counting the rows and seats. *Hope they're not short,* he thought and grinned. Finally, he reached the very first row and the raised stage was in front of him.

He realized that this meant he now had to work too, so he took stock of what the stage held, its location, its facilities, and its ambush or danger points.

It was about eighty feet wide by about forty feet deep, he guessed, as his first job was to walk all the way around same. Not a problem at first, but behind the stage, things were tight. The audio-visual team had their own setup there, followed by some techies who looked like IT types. Scaffolding went up and up and held the huge display screen above the stage—it too was about the same eighty feet wide. Cables lay everywhere, snaking into generators that ran silently or back into the tower itself via conduit ports. He carefully stepped over them all and made the far side of the rear of the stage.

Up the last side and he had finished his first job, which was learning what he was facing in respect to the stage. There were flights of stairs—six stairs, he noted—on the left side, and the right side, and a huge triple-wide set was at the rear too. More than enough to allow the heads of state and their entourages of guards to get access to the stage.

He then took a flight of those stairs up and walked the whole stage. He checked every single chair and even got down on all fours to look down the rows to confirm that not even one had any kind of package under same. *Bad package*, he meant, but then he realized that anyone putting a package below a chair would need to know who was in that chair.

He rose, and went to the back, and looked at the backs of all the chairs.

Yup. Each had a large placard with the name of the head of state to be seated in that chair, but all had been artfully placed so that from in front you couldn't see same.

The Doge of Conclusion, the three admirals, the Baroness, and Professor Watkins were all in the first row on the left side.

The same front row over on the right held RIM Confederacy Chairman Gramsci, the Duke d'Avigdor, the Master Adept, and the Eran.

He noted that the row just behind that front row was short by two seats, and that did get a grin out of him.

Well back, after about a ten-foot-wide space, were just plain rows for the heads of state guards—no names, of course.

He smiled.

Good. Seating is fine. Now to look for attack centers, and he turned to look out toward the audience.

No elevated spots. Not a single vantage point for a sniper to sit and take slow, quiet aim. The only spot for that would be in the front row, and even then, there was no way to get a Merkel or any kind of a carbine or rifle into play—they were just far too big and long.

So it'd need to be a handgun, stunner, or needler-type hand weapon. And to make sure you got your quarry with a hand weapon, you had to be pretty damn close. The front row was twenty feet away. That would mean that any attacker would need to rush the stage.

Fine.

He left the area and searched and found a Provost guard who nicely offered to get the Provost captain in charge and bring him over to the stage area.

He waited a few minutes, sitting on a chair in the front row, and soon the Provost captain came over.

"Sir?" he asked as he snapped a salute to Tanner.

Surprised, Tanner said, "Captain, I'm the same rank as you—no need to salute me at all," and instead he held out his hand.

Surprised, the Provost captain grasped it and shook it well.

"Sorry, Sir—we all know who you are, so it's just a sign of respect for those eagles, Sir," he said, noting the standard rank insignia for a captain was the pair of eagles in Tanner's collar.

"Provost … I am thinking that the heads of state are very well protected with the stage setup and its access points. But what does worry me is that, with the first row only twenty feet back, someone who was armed with a hand weapon could charge the stage to perhaps get off at least a shot or two," he said, as he pointed at the row and then the stage.

The Provost captain nodded. "Sir, if I could? Maybe I can station, say, four Provost guards—two per each side in chairs so that they do not block any view-lines? They'd be armed, of course, and if nothing else, such a display would—"

"Would make any attacker think twice. Yes, I agree, Provost. That would be a good thing to do," Tanner interrupted.

Both captains nodded to each other, and the Provost guard moved off to get that job done.

Sitting again in the front row, Tanner thought of all the other items he knew had come to pass in the past five months.

While he was lost in that area, his PDA flashed at him, and the AI gave him a monochromatic teal blue hologram of the Lady St. August.

"Tanner, know you're busy, so I just wanted to leave you this message. Spoke to the Baroness who is on Ghayth right now, and she said that she'd be here for the opening—so I need another seat for me, I'd guess. How she can get to Eons in a couple of hours is beyond my ken … but she did say you'd know and that she's on the *Atlas* too. See you around lunchtime—I hear that they have some Oved Kimchi that is to die for! Bye, honey!" her message finished off, and he archived it for later.

There was only one way that the Baroness could be on Ghayth and get to Eons—some sixty-five lights—in a couple of hours, and that was to use the new Barony Drive. That was interesting, he thought and went off a moment on what that would mean once the RIM found out about this new instant travel option. One that the Barony only had so far ... but at least the Atlas would be here, hoping to touch base with the best crew in any man's navy.

He nodded to himself and said, "Back to today."

Today we open up the new academy—wait, he suddenly thought. I wonder what will happen to the old academy buildings and complex. Should be useful to someone. He glanced at his PDA to see that he'd been here almost an hour.

And only four more hours to go until the academy opening event kick-off. He would have to go into the administration tower to find something to do, he expected.

#####

It seemed like a month later rather than hours later when Tanner took his seat in the last seat on the left in the front row. Before him, and facing outward toward the audience, were three of those Provost guards, all nicely sitting up and looking professional. Each was armed, and nobody could miss the big handguns on their hips. Each guard was studying the crowd ahead of them.

While the stage had featured specific seating for the heads of state and other guests, the audience was a first come, first choice deal, so beside Tanner was a family. A dad, mom, little girl, and a cadet in uniform—human too, he noted, sat next to him. He smiled at the parents and chuckled as the little girl got up and danced a bit sometimes when the audio-visual team had music on the system.

He leaned forward and looked all the way down the first row, which was a long way away, and there was nothing out of order as far as he could tell.

The audience was composed mostly of cadets and their families, and it was a happy boisterous group.

On the enormous vid screen above the stage, a series of short vids were playing in a loop. Each went to a different tower, and each showed the progress that had been made from bare I-Beams and concrete floors to fully finished student residence rooms, lecture halls, gyms, and quartermaster stores. *Someone pretty good had done a great job of showing off the four towers,* and Tanner was proud he'd been able to help a bit too. While there was no sound track, music played behind the vids.

The Provost captain had spoken to the guards he'd posted at least at this end of the stage—they knew who Tanner was and had been told in case of emergency, he was the one to look to.

Good idea. Should have thought of that one myself, he thought as the heads of state were now coming up the back stairs and taking their seats on

276

stage. While they were not filing on in any kind of order, he was pleased to see that an extra chair had been tucked into the left side of the front row to seat Helena. The Doge and all three admirals were already ensconced, and the Baroness entered and was, as usual, a vision in abalone. Like the inside of an oyster, the iridescent shine was coming off her hair with sparkles, off her short cut-away jacket, and her boots too. She was, without a doubt, a beautiful woman, and Tanner nodded to her and got a nod back. Moments later, the Lady St. August took the seat between the Baroness and the professor, and that half row was complete. Helena was in coral, and her hair was exactly the same shade as her heels and her handbag, while her leggings were pure white. Tanner almost whistled, and then he nodded and got a nod back—she also blew him a kiss.

He blushed. Anyone paying attention would have seen that kiss.

He looked away and then back and noted that the other half row had already seated themselves while Tanner had been noticing the two women from the Barony.

One thing, he knew, was that admirals, like all navy men, believed in time lines, and as his PDA chimed thirteen hundred hours, Admiral Childs rose and walked forward to the microphone placed on the center of the stage lectern.

He tapped the mic three times, and by the third time, the sound for the vid loops was leveled off.

"Heads of state of the RIM Confederacy, honored guests, ladies and gentlemen of all races, and cadets—let me welcome you to the new RIM Confederacy Naval Academy grand opening event!"

This got a huge response from the cadets, cheers and huzzahs and even a couple of tossed hats went up as Tanner partially turned to look behind him at the two thousand attendees.

Going to be a long day if this crowd cheers at a welcome, he thought and turned back to the stage.

Admiral Childs went on, and Tanner remembered not a single speaker had been told to limit their remarks to any set timeline. He spoke of the challenges to the new builds and of the great architects and construction firms that had done their best to get the construction to today.

That got an even bigger cheer, and he had to wait until the almost two thousand cadets quieted down.

He went on about what that would mean, with the doubling of the number of academy graduates every year, and how that would help all of the RIM Confederacy member navies. More cheers.

He did smile though at the end, looked down, and checked the Agenda. A copy of the Agenda had been pasted on the lectern top so that the speaker would always know who he or she was supposed to introduce.

"It is now my pleasure—my very great pleasure—to introduce the Issian Master Adept for her comments on today's opening," he said, as he looked over to the front row to his left and gestured for the Master to take the lectern.

She got up slowly and made her way over to the lectern, and the admiral pushed the mic on its flexible stand somewhat lower so that she could use it easily.

She nodded to the admiral, cleared her throat, and then something strange happened.

A trilling sound echoed as the enormous video screen above the stage faded to black.

He instantly thought that the audio-visual crew had an issue and hoped they could get it straightened out immediately.

And then a woman's face came on the vid screen, and she looked down at them all.

He knew then that there was an attack, but it was a tech one. As the woman began to speak, a crawl along the bottom with big neon yellow warning icons began. He bounced up and out of his seat and almost missed the part that said that the cables with power had been rigged and were live, not to touch them, and this was a four-minute video.

He ran down the left-hand side of the stage, noting that all the heads of state had turned to look up at the video playing above their heads. As he got to the end of the stage and rounded to his right, he found the Provost captain was there already and screaming at the audio-visual team.

"What do you mean, it's not you guys?"

The team leader held out his hands, palms up, and said, "Not coming from us—the academy IT has been hacked. This is a feed from somewhere else." He looked up at the back of the screen on the huge scaffolding.

"The crawl says too that the cables to the screen are rigged—else I'd say just pull the plug on the whole screen," he added, but even Tanner could tell that he didn't know what to believe.

On a monitor on the audio-visual console desk, the vid screen was showing the face of the woman doing the talking, and Tanner felt a lot better as the face faded away.

But like many of the audience just beyond the stage, he was suddenly presented with what looked like a patient in a room in a hospital. She was tied to the bed. She had hair that had not been combed in months. The length and curling of her long, long fingernails and toenails was more than apparent, and she looked like she weighed less than ninety pounds. As the patient tossed and slowly turned toward the camera, he realized they were going to see her face. She had a bloody temple and a scrape along one ear, and as she suddenly thrust her head at the camera, Tanner gasped.

He heard the audience out front gasp loudly too.

The woman was an identical twin of the woman who'd spoken to them before, and she was now slowly fading back into the screen as the patient room disappeared.

She spoke one more time, and it was burned into Tanner's consciousness.

"I ask the gathered heads of state," she said, "to launch an investigation into this Issian terrorist program ... the killing of a twin over and over ... to make the rulers of Eons that much stronger. This must not be allowed ..."

Christ. What a mess.

He turned and charged back to the same side of the stage, reached the edge, and said to the Provost guards who were now all standing up, ready for whatever came next, "Caution here, lads ... no mistakes, but then again, we know our duty."

He finally looked up on stage and saw that the Master Adept had frozen at the lectern and had now turned forward to face the audience.

And not a sound came from the thousands out there. Not a scream or a yell or a catcall—the audience had taken this in and as yet hadn't voiced anything back.

And suddenly, the Baroness was at the Master Adept's side, and she pulled the microphone back up so that she could use it and spoke softly and very, very respectfully.

She acknowledged the audience and heads of states first and simply said, "I would like to speak about that video, if you all will permit me?"

She didn't wait, however, for any okays, and she just went on.

"I do not know if what we just saw is true. Or not. I do know that the patient we did see looks like —well, yes, like a twin for this Kendal Steyn. And I want to know more, so, Kendal," she said, staring at the row of media folks and cameramen off to the side, "I make you this offer. The Barony will offer you sanctuary, and we will be pleased to include all of your group too. We will provide you full immunity to allow us to take you, and anyone else you want, to plead your case at the next RIM Confederacy Council meeting in about a month and a half. They will listen and they will decide if what they hear does amount to this terrorism you accuse the Issians of—or not. If those terms are agreeable, then simply contact me via our embassy over in Dessau, and I will make all that happen. It is the best thing, I think, to air out these charges and get to the truth.

The Master Adept nodded beside her, and there was quiet all over the stage after she said "and I concur."

Then the Doge of Conclusion and the Chairman Gramsci of the Confederacy Council rose and began to clap their hands. Every other head of state then did the same, and the applause grew to now include the audience itself.

Cadets threw up more hats, and once again, the event changed its tone. The Baroness took the Master Adept back over to her chair and had her sit.

Professor Nigel Watkins, nonplussed by what had just happened, strode up to the microphone. He made his two-minute talk about how happy the professorial union was with the new academy and sat.

There was no way Professor Watkins would have missed his opportunity to speak, no matter what had just happened. Tanner saw that Superintendent Chapman spoke to Admiral Childs and must have gotten a good to go, as he then approached the lectern and made his speech. It was nice, as he actually congratulated the admirals—all three of them—on their help and attention to detail.

The cadets yelled, "Woo-hoo," and even Tanner had to think that this was a bit self-serving, but he dipped his head to Chapman at the end of the man's few minutes and received a grin in return.

Admiral Higgins reciprocated with the same kind of kudos to the construction firm as well, and finally Admiral McQueen took the lectern. He waved at a couple of ensigns, and they each went to one end of the stage, holding between them a long blue and gold ribbon with the dagger icon of the RIM Confederacy Navy on same.

A few more ensigns made their way between the heads of state, who all stood and took a spot somewhere along the long ribbon. Once all the heads of state were armed with scissors, the admiral finally spoke.

"Well, it's been an interesting day to be sure. But while some of the things we've been told today await verification later—one thing I can assure you of is this. The Academy will be officially open as soon as our collection here of RIM Confederacy heads of state do the last thing—cut the ribbon, please!" he said, and almost together, each of the heads cut the ribbon.

The audience swelled and hundreds of hats went up into the air. Shouts of woo-hoo echoed throughout the audience, and there wasn't a seated audience member or stage guest.

Tanner grinned up at Helena and she grinned back.

Even the Baroness smiled down at him too.

One thing he thought of then was that at no time had he succumbed to the PTSD that must still be within him. And he said to himself, "I never even used the one, two two ... one, two two pattern of EMDR that worked for me in the past."

He was not cured.

But this event—as traumatic as it had been—hadn't sent him into a spin.

Good to know, he thought, as the cadets and their families now slowly went to the back of the tarmac to enjoy the catering and the bars.

As he turned back, he noted that the Master Adept had taken her seat again and just stared off at the backs of the audience well in the distance. She looks lost in thought, he thought. Wonder how much of what this Kendal had offered could be proven ... or not ...

#####

He squirmed just a bit on the chair and realized that the admiral had not meant to disparage the audio-visual team, yet somehow Higgins felt that yesterday's events were someone's fault.

"Dunno who opened up the event to this kind of hacker intrusion—but someone is to blame," he said, as he pointed at Tanner.

"But that's not going to be your worry anymore, Captain," he said as he rifled through the folders on his desk and found the one he was looking for. He opened same and nodded as he pulled out a sheaf of folded papers and handed them over.

"As of oh nine hundred hours today, you're hereby discharged of the duties you were charged with, what, five months ago. That also includes what was supposed to be the first semester of teaching too. We were going to put you into Aerial Combat Tactics, I believe, but that's moot now," he said as he handed over the sheaf of orders.

Tanner didn't look at them but tilted his head at Higgins.

"Sir—can I ask why my orders were changed?"

"No idea, Captain—but I was told to tell you to report to the Baroness over on the *Atlas* at fifteen hundred hours later today. Those orders just release you—I've no idea where you're off to, Captain."

"I've also taken the liberty of letting Admirals McQueen and Childs know about this too—I know that once you do find out, you will let them know too?" he said, as he stood and held out his hand.

"Captain—loved having you a part of this— should have asked earlier. Wherever you do end up, I know you'll be fine," he said, and Tanner shook his hand gratefully.

Having an admiral—well, maybe three admirals —who liked you and your abilities was a good thing to have.

He left and made sure to say goodbye to the admiral's aide, Lieutenant CoSharan, and he promised to yes, let him know too where he ended up.

Packing was pretty easy, figuring that the *Sterling* could drop him off somewhere on his trip to his next assignment, and he had a steward run his bags over to Helena's ship.

He couldn't resist, and he took up that blue flyer for one more trip out to the academy towers, and he made a loop around each before heading back to Dessau.

He turned in his Eons IDs, got a thanks from some clerk at the quartermaster's station, and then walked over to the *Sterling*. But before he got there, he sat on a dolly that wasn't in use on the tarmac and used his PDA to send out some messages. First to Kondo and he received a "yup, will see you this aft" response, which meant that Kondo knew he'd be aboard later. He messaged Professor Watkins, thanked him for his comments yesterday, and wished him luck with the next class. He messaged Superintendent Chapman too and thanked him for the help in getting the towers up and ready.

He sat in the sunshine, his eyes closed and head tilted back, and just enjoyed the late spring day.

#####

As he went to the boarding ramp on the *Atlas*, he got a real grin from a lieutenant he barely knew and was passed through and onto the ship in a few seconds.

All the lieutenant had said was that the Baroness would see him in her quarters.

This meant he had to go up to Deck Four, almost above the bridge itself, to what was called the Royal Quarters.

It was three times the size of the captain's quarters, and as he remembered, it had the softest of carpets, the walls adorned with art, and the couch looked like you'd need to be a Royal just to sit in same.

He slowly walked Deck Five, stopping every so often to say hello to crew that he knew. There were some new ones he didn't know, but he got the biggest of smiles and kudos from one and all. It was a long way from the boarding port up to the final set of stairs up to Deck Four, and he took them two at a time.

Turning forward once more, he went right up to the Royal Quarters door and spoke to the AI.

"Ship's AI—this is Captain Scott, seeking permission to enter," he said, and moments later, the door slid open.

Inside was a foyer, followed by a small butler's

pantry area that then opened up into a huge great room with many seating groups of couches and love seats.

At one on the left, the Baroness sat, bouncing a bare foot on her crossed legs, and she smiled up at him.

Sitting to her left, the Lady St. August sat also barefooted, and he wondered who had had the duty of painting each toenail those different shades of what appeared to be green—and then not green too.

He smiled and took a seat on the edge of a love seat and turned all his attention to the Baroness.

She nodded and took a sip of what looked like some kind of sparkling wine and said very, very softly, "Welcome, Admiral."

She reached forward, slid a velvet box in the Barony blue and red with the twin crowns on the top across the table between them, and then leaned back. He looked over at Helena who had not a single thing on her face, just a blank stare at him.

He picked up the box and opened it. Yes, there were two silver stars meaning that the one wearing these would hold the rank of rear admiral.

He closed the box and yet didn't put it back down on the table instead he grasped it tightly in his hand.

He looked over at Helena.

"This your doing, Ma'am?" he asked quietly.

She looked at the Baroness and said, "See, told you. No, Admiral, this has nothing to do with me—this is an honor from the Baroness entirely. Ask her," she said, and so he looked at the Baroness.

She nodded and took another big sip of her sparkling wine.

"Admiral, yes, I thought that as you're going to be marrying the heir to the Barony—you'd need at least a star—maybe more," she said, and once again, Tanner blushed and his gaze whipped over to Helena.

"I didn't have to say anything, Tanner—she knew," Helena responded, and he nodded at that.

He had learned that trying to keep something like his staying nights on the *Sterling* would be a lost cause—obviously.

"Ma'am," he said to the Baroness, "I also received a discharge on my original orders to come to Eons and help with construction and then remain to teach the first semester. Might I inquire as to what my new orders will be?"

The Baroness looked surprised. "Admiral—you now run the whole Barony Navy. You decide what you want to do, where you want to go. Yes, there will be missions that you will be given—but as the admiral, you can do them yourself or give it to others too. Is this not how a navy works?" she asked, and he had to nod back to her. She had that right.

"As well, one thing I can tell you is that this ship, the *Atlas*, will be your flagship—same Captain Lazaro, but he'll do all the work of running your flagship—and the reports too. I understand that's a real bane of any captain's existence. But an admiral doesn't have to do any of that. Will that suffice for your own ship, Admiral," she asked, and he grinned right back at her.

"Plus, you will now also take over the Captains Council—your fleet, your captains—you run them as you will. Oh, here's a word for you to remember, Admiral—delegate. Learn to delegate ..."

He nodded, as it made sense, and continued to listen.

"As you probably know, this ship was on Ghayth just this morning. Yes, we used the new Barony Drive to get to Eons—took I think, what, eleven seconds. We are covering that flight and all other *Atlas* flights with the story that we have upgraded the Tachyon Drives with the Seenra—very hush-hush, you should say, but then what isn't when you sit at the top of the heap," she added that aside and sipped again. And again.

"We will make the necessary notices to the Barony Navy and announce same at an upcoming RIM Confederacy Council meeting too. We will leave it to you to take care of the *Atlas* crew and

Captains Council. Will that suffice?"

He nodded but then stopped. "Ma'am, you started this conversation with the notice that you know that … that Helena and I are in love. And we intend to marry, but at this point, Ma'am, we have not discussed—"

She held up a hand. "Admiral, if there is one thing you must know, it's that the groom gets no part of the planning," she said, and it was as if he suddenly was not even in the room. She turned instead to Helena and smiled.

"Dear, have you as yet even thought about a date?"

"Ma'am, yes, in about a year we thought," Helena said.

"Location?" the Baroness asked.

"Well, we were hoping—"

The Baroness interrupted Helena and both nodded and grinned at her. "Helena, we'd like—the Barony would like—to host your wedding at the Barony Palace. We'll build a whole new wing for you two, and it will be the biggest and best wedding the RIM has ever seen. Ten thousands guests, every single head of state, all the RIM Council members too. We can do this up superbly."

She nodded and Tanner could tell that he had really no say at all.

Not a blessed thing.

"Oh, your bridal party—any idea how big you want that?"

Helena shook her head and said. "Let me think on that one ..."

And the talk went on.

It took about an hour for them to discuss everything from which botanist to approach to create their own wedding flowers to which vid service to stream the wedding all over the RIM.

An admiral, he thought. At forty.

Wonder how far this could go. He made sure his eyes didn't glaze over when they began to talk about swag for the guests and if a centerpiece for a table valued at one thousand credits seemed big enough.

And he squeezed that box of stars...

Epilogue ~

As he slowly turned over, he had his eyes shut tight in case Helena was awake.

He figured that if he looked like he was asleep, she'd not wake him with more questions.

The three of them had sat for almost three hours in the Royal Quarters, and he'd heard more about the wedding than he ever wanted to know. Just get a ladder and elope was his answer.

Marry at a city hall on some RIM planet somewhere.

Find a small spot and raise some kids.

The squint that he held his eyes closed in strengthened.

There was no way that this was going to be a simple life anymore.

Admiral, he thought.

I'm an admiral and got my first star.

Will need a great aide. Will need an understanding with Kondo too—the ship is his. I just tell him where to take me.

No reports, and at that he almost grinned, and that would tell Helena he was awake if she was watching his face.

So he squelched that and thought about a whole bunch of odds and ends.

The Barony Drive—it'd get out pretty damn

soon; he'd have to find a way to monitor that story.

The Kendal thing with the terrorist claims against the Issian Inner Circle. Next month in Juno.

The Caliph and the unending hate tween the Caliphate and the Barony.

The Ikarian longevity virus and it's vaccine.

Ghayth and it's hidden future to the Barony.

What he was going to do about his friendships with Bram and Alver and Kondo too was something more to think on.

What might be happening over on Leudi—had there not been some kind of vid that some ships had been seized?

He had to remember that he was the new head of the Barony Navy—that for the issues around the RIM Navy, he only could care and look after so much.

He remembered that he was also supposed to delegate too.

He jammed an arm into the edge of his pillow to pop it up a bit to ease his neck, but he wasn't able to get it right.

So he opened up his eyes and was able to punch the edge just right.

He saw Helena was staring directly at him, and she half-smiled at him.

"Sleep, Admiral, you need sleep ..." and he drifted off…

Eons Semester

Eons Semester

BOOK NINE OF THE RIM CONFEDERACY

Trade Wars

Prologue ~

Jinni wailed and as the Assistant Assistant Port Keeper looked over towards her cage he could see her back sail standing straight up. Leudies again, he said to himself as he tried not to give in to the frustration felt every time they landed.

Out on the Merilda Landing Port tarmac, he could see the faint glow growing on pad 23. They'd made good time coming down from orbit once they'd gotten the automatic okay and landing pad assignment but then Leudies always made good time, he thought, which is another reason they're good traders. Now that gold glow was turning a deeper red, and you could hear the growing sound of their thrusters in the atmosphere – at least they hadn't come down on antimatter pulses. They'd been known to lift off on same and had paid dear penalties the next time they landed though Wiggins admitted that had been almost 1 sol year ago. And they sure didn't like paying any landing penalties he knew as he gathered up the forms that they'd have to fill in on their landing here on Merilda. We're not the most advanced port, but we do our tasks honestly, he did feel was true.

Out on the tarmac, the scooter was taking out Customs, Duties and Health to check their cargo manifests and behind them an empty transport with off loaders chugged out to offload that cargo if it was allowed in.

Hmmmph, Wiggins thought, Leudies always got their cargo in and made good credits deal after deal.

After all, as a trading race, these aliens worked at making deals all across the RIM, from UrPoPo almost 80 lightyears distant to Eran. They traded for one thing on one planet, moved to where it was badly needed and drew a hard bargain with the needy and made credits on both ends. Sometimes, Wiggins thought as he smiled, they didn't do so well, but even though they were not well liked, they usually made a profit no matter at whose expense.

That Crux Epidermis plague of two years ago had come from inward, and had threatened to eat away the skin of every RIM Confederacy citizen it found – and the Leudies had moved the latest serum from more than 300 lightyears inward at quite a cost to themselves for both energy and lost time and had been able to get the serum to all who'd need it on time at a fair profit. Course, then they'd made a much bigger fatter profit on what had happened next.

All the people no matter what species who had used the serum, broke down shortly afterward with a full depression, induced it was said due to blood – or what passed for blood – chemistry changes via that serum. So the Leudies had also bought the rights for the anti-serum you then had to take to get rid of the depression you got from the original cure. They made a fortune on that – far more than on the original serum and of course they'd never told anyone about the depression side-effects either.

Leudies were not liked much nor respected much, Wiggins knew as he heard the sound of their boots climbing the 3 stairs to the Port Keeper's Office. Glancing at Jinni, he could see she had wrapped herself up in a ball after trying to dig under her nest in the corner of the cage. Something about Leudies made her react this way every time one came into the Port Keepers offices and he wondered maybe if he should look that up later in Gallipedia, as he put on a bland smile, squared around his simple uniform shirt and faced the door, paperwork in hand.

"Right, we're here and we're not paying these exorbitant fees," the first Leudie through the door stated loudly, as his cloak brushed the door sill and he moved in towards the counter.

Wiggins could tell by the forest green of that cloak that this was the Captain. He was tall for a Leudie, almost 2 meters and built as solid as they all were. On his head rode the Captains toque that was usual attire for a trader, the Captains double gold bars polished and bright. On his legs were what could only be called some kind of leggings, thin flesh-hugging green pants like they all wore and on his chest beneath the green cloak Wiggins could see the brass colored shirt. While Leudies were humanoids, they were a colorful bunch, he thought.

"Never," said his First Mate, who followed his Captain in tandem and who also wore the Leudie green cloak but in a lighter shade than the Captain's darker color. He grabbed the paperwork out of Wiggin's hands and began to jot down the data needed, a sneer on his lips.

"What's more," the Captain now almost shouted, "we are always appalled at the backwards-ness of this planet and its outdated and antiquated Port landing systems. If Merilda wasn't a hub for mining equipment trading, we would have gone right through to Duos," he added.

"Right!" the First Mate chimed in, still

scrabbling answers to the declaration papers.

"Imagine," the Captain said, "we have to fill out a paper form here just to let a squad of your longshoremen unload our cargo – by hand!" The Captain was busy taking off his gloves to reveal soft and supple hands that had rings on almost every finger. Wiggins cleared his throat before the First Mate could chime in.

"Understood, Captain. Your comments – such as they are – will be relayed to the RIM Confederacy Council when they meet next. Till then, I'm afraid that you must yes, fill in these forms by hand. May I see the Customs, Duties and Health receipts please?" Wiggins held out his hand, awaiting the paperwork from Customs and Health that would certify the cargo and indicate any and all duties or taxes or even quarantines that would have to be paid or followed.

The Leudie Captain glared at Wiggins, his hand stroking at his neck.

"And who exactly might you be? Some junior junior clerk whose only real job here is to feed your ugly balled-up Carnelian Lizard" he said as he snorted and petted the coiled rope of muscle that surrounded his neck. Wiggins thought that the coil twitched for a moment, but knew that a Leudie neck Snake would never uncoil unless it was hungry or wanted affection. Each Leudie had one of these "pets" Wiggins thought given to them at puberty and the two of them formed a pair bond that was unbreakable it was said, wrapped around its owner's neck is how the creature spent its life.

"I am the Assistant Assistant Port Keeper, Captain," Wiggins replied.

"Ah, yes! You're the little clerk who seemed to think that we were exporting food items and wanted us to pay taxes on those passengers!" The Captain actually smiled down at Wiggins, and pointed a multi-ringed finger directly into his face.

"But when we appealed, your boss and even RIM Customs agreed with us, didn't they little assistant assistant Port Keeper! They knew what we were doing was well within the legal limits – too bad that was beyond you. Could have saved you much embarrassment, eh?" the Captain gloated, his voice now soft and cloying as he shook his finger in Wiggins face.

Wiggins shuffled the papers before him, riding tight rein on his embarrassment. I mean after all he thought, if you buy seafood, even live seafood from a fish distributor here on Juno, and then try to weasel out of paying your fair share of taxes by using the excuse that you were just transporting passengers to DenKoss, a water world only 16 light-years away, anybody should have seen through that. The fact that the buyers on DenKoss swore that they were just trying to liberate some of their like species, didn't hold water at all – yet the Leudies had been able to force through their exemption and the fees that Wiggins had originally charged, were negated. Score one for the Leudies.

"That's right – you were the Assistant Assistant who tried to penalize us for that little stopover to pick up passengers here. That was most unfair, and as you most likely heard, we had nothing at all to do with the fact that once situated in their new home, all of the passengers became food stuffs for the local population of DenKoss royalty. We didn't know that, of course, so we're not to blame, right little clerk?" The Captain leaned down on the counter; his face was now a light gray in color which for a blue-skinned Leudie meant that he found something funny. He stomped his foot, the boot heel smacking the wooden floor with a loud bang!

"Well, little clerk, what do you have to say about that mistake in judgment?" he said, as he roared.

"Actually, Captain, you know yourself that while you can touchdown on any of the planets out here on the RIM, if you off-load or on-load anything, you may be taxed on those items. And I was only following our laws here when I taxed you on the on-loaded seafood that you took to DenKoss. And as it sounds, I was right wasn't I?" Wiggins looked up directly at the Leudie, whose finger still speared at his face, his laughter subsiding.

"Not in the slightest, little clerk. We move things around; we don't care what they are as long as there is a profit attached. It's bureaucrats like you who do the worrying. And on this trip we're again looking to add to our cargo, so no more mistakes, clerk!" He smiled down at Wiggins again, and gathered up his gloves as his First Mate slid the paperwork over and in front of Wiggins and then tugged at the hem of his Captains cloak.

"Let's go, Captain. This one's too unimportant to even gloat over..." and he had finished up the forms and then opened the door to leave the office.

"Far too unimportant – most likely as I figured, he's just the lizard's caregiver....and as ugly as his charge as well," the Captain said as he stroked his neck Snake and twirled the cloak around him as he tromped down the stairs and back out onto the tarmac while Wiggins fumed.

He fussed with their paperwork and thought while he was over there at Customs, he'd take a moment to look up Carnelian Lizards and why they reacted so badly to Leudies as he closed the folder...wait till they find out about the new charges for mining equipment and the Faraway subsidies....

Available in the Summer of 2016!

Want to get early notice when we've got a new RIM Confederacy Series book launch?

Just drop by www.jimrudnick.ca and leave you email address and we'll let you know!

Or drop by our Face Book page at www.facebook.com/theRIMConfederacy/

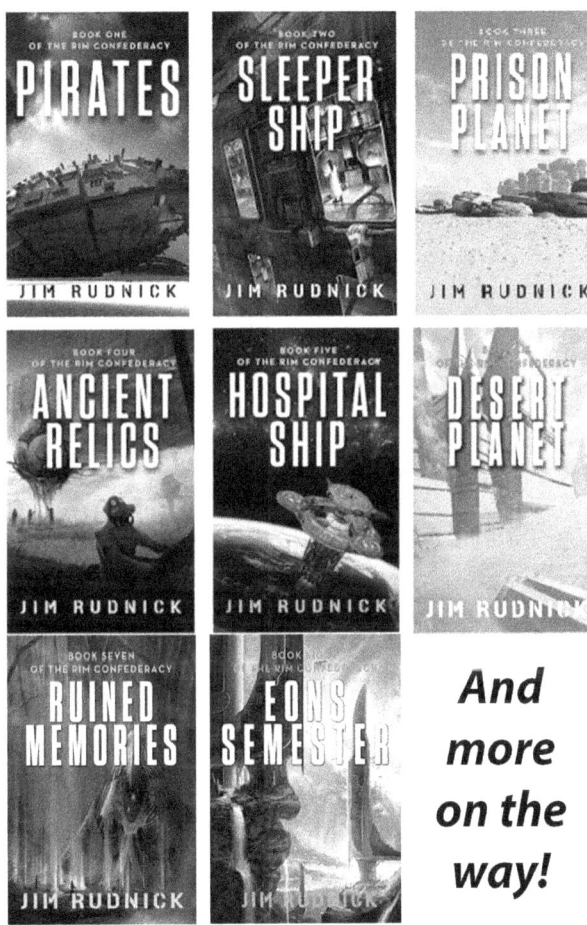

Dear Reader...

If you've made it this far, you're most likely thinking that this was the best SciFi you've ever read.

Or maybe not.

Maybe Captain Scott wasn't your cup of tea?

Or you hate the Baroness and her scheming ways?

Or does the Caliph look like an upcoming tyrant?

Or the Issian mind-readers are suspect?

So...I'd like to ask you for a favor?

Would you mind taking a few minutes to write a review for me please?

And I'm talking honest too! Nothing makes us writers get better than book reviews!

Your comments help others know what to expect when they're looking for a great SciFi read...

And thanks once again, I'm looking

Eons Semester

forward to reading your comments!

Jim Rudnick
2016